MAGNETIC

A Reverse Harem Shifter Romance

ANYA J COSGROVE

Magnetic

Cover designer: Fiona Jayde Media

Magnetic/Anya J Cosgrove

ISBN 978-1-9993901-8-1

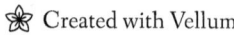 Created with Vellum

"Sweetheart, my last boyfriend was a homicidal lizard, so I think I can handle a werewolf."
-Lydia Martin (Teen Wolf)

KISS WITH A FIST

VICKY

A girl needs a lot of sugar to heal her broken heart.

"Large chocolate caramel mochaccino, extra-extra foam, please," I say, searching my skirt's pocket for a ten dollar bill. Organic, eco-friendly sugar is expensive.

There's no line behind me, so the barista is in no hurry. She gawks at my shimmering braid as she prepares my *getting-over-a-guy* drink, pouring a bit of foam to the side. The misplaced bubbles splash to the counter, but she's too busy checking me out to notice. A big blackboard towers behind her, her fingers white with chalk. When a trickle of caramel sauce splatters on her flats, she curses, finally looking away.

Even when I'm muted, humans react to my lure. Her hazel pupils are dilated, and her chest is flushed. Usually, it'd give me a boost of confidence, but not today.

She leans closer and hands me the plastic cup. "Here you go."

Sweat and coffee beans tickle my nose, the slightest hint of arousal lurking behind them. Her gaze darts to my ass.

"Thank you." I grab my drink and avoid touching her hand, sparing her the mind-numbing horniness that would follow if our fingers were to brush.

I slurp my coffee and sit on a stool, my shoulders hunched. The spring in my step is missing; I should offer a reward for its return.

Getting dumped sucks. Sex demons don't get dumped. It doesn't happen. Vandellas never get dumped. We tire out our prey and move on. Being cast aside by my favorite lover *and* his brother in the same summer just blows. Why do Walker men care about monogamy, anyway? It's so overrated.

If my succubus friends knew about this... It's so humiliating.

A guy stops next to me, and I glance up from my drink.

"Hey," he says, his eyes lingering on the scruffy hem of denim at my mid-thigh.

He's got blond hair, a chiseled jaw, and nice strong shoulders. He's super hot, but I don't care. *Me*, the girl who feeds on sex.

"Hey," I answer half-heartedly.

"You're not from around here, are you?"

I snort. "No, I'm not."

I'm thousands of miles away from where I was born, with no intention to ever return. No wonder I don't fit in with Americans—or humans in general.

"I'm Jace." He extends his hand, and the edge of a tattoo peeks from under his sleeve.

I bat my eyelashes without touching him. "Hi, Jace. I'm Vicky, and normally I'd do you, but I'm having a real bad day."

His eyes are wide at my brazenness.

I get that a lot. It's hard to be proper when you know all the dirty desires and wicked fantasies people hide beneath layers of denial. I might not be a witch, but I sure can read human emotions better than most. Between the blood rushing to his ears and the abrupt bob of his Adam's apple, I'm pretty sure Jace is confused by his raging erection.

I wave my hand for him to leave, and he staggers to the cash register, adjusting his pants.

Still... I'm hungry. Vandellas need to feed almost every day. It doesn't have to be the whole nine yards, but sexual energy is my chicken, rice and carrots. A great kiss is like munching on a bag of chips. Second base is French fries and a Coke. A good sensual massage equates to a nice healthy salad.

Human sex packs enough calories for a day. Good demon action is the dirtiest of feasts and keeps me going for thirty-so hours, forty when I'm really into the guy.

And I also need food and water, so it's no wonder I don't have time to save the world or get a real job.

The worst part about my day is that I got dumped *before* sex. I never expected my latest fling to last long—the man was a boy scout at heart, but he couldn't even do the guy thing and wait until *after* we fucked to break the news, and I have to eat today.

Bag of chips it is. In three strides, I've caught up with Jace. Before he can say anything, I grip his collar and plant my lips on his. The mint tucked behind his teeth clashes with the taste of coffee, but I soldier through, his mouth hot and pliant against mine. He encircles my waist, desire surging through him. A low moan rumbles at the back of his throat, and he whimpers when I pull away.

"Nice kiss, Jace. I'd recommend you to a friend." I wink and turn on my heels.

Humans generally take minutes to rationalize what happened.

I steal kisses, but never sex. Sex needs to be fun for both parties, and I'm not about to force myself on a human. Sure, I give them a nice sample of what I'm offering, but I always, always mute myself and give them a chance to say no. Few men ever say no.

Still. I'm tired. Men are too predictable, and the ones that aren't prefer to chase after girls that keep them waiting. Playing hard to get isn't my forte.

Demons are mostly the same. They fight to upstage one another for the honor of being my favorite conquest. They're self-conscious of their performance, hoping their stamina will be praised to future generations. My ex was different.

Tears mist over my eyes, but I will them away. We didn't work, so I'm glad he found something real.

I could kill the bitch.

A relentless sun scorches the recently paved parking lot, the black asphalt shimmering. I shrug off my jacket and wipe sweat off my forehead with the sleeves. My frilly top is tied right below my breasts, leaving my stomach bare, and a gentle breeze coming from the trees at the back of the lot cools me down.

Raised voices become more and more audible as I near the green Jeep I stole earlier. A teenage girl wearing a barista uniform is arguing with a man with squared shoulders and a cheap tattoo.

"Come on, baby, you can't keep torturing me like this." The man grabs her arm a little too strongly for my taste, and I pause. He looks older than her by at least ten years.

"I have to go to work," she says, fleeing from his grasp. She walks around a big wood bench towards the employee's back door.

He stops her a few feet short from her goal and pins her to the wall. "I'll get you at nine. We can go to my place. I'll show you a good time, babe."

Her mouth curls down. "I told you. I'm not ready for any of that yet. Brianna is picking me up."

His cajoling tones vanishes. "You're no virgin, so what's the problem? Scared to handle a real man?" He pinches her ass and hikes her skirt up.

The girl shoves his hand off her, but he steps between her legs.

When he crushes his mouth to hers, I leap in their direction. "Hey!"

"Mind your own business—" The wannabe rapist stops, his jaw slack. They were both too busy to notice me before, but now I've got their attention.

I put my jacket down on the bench and take a deep breath. "Do you need help?"

The girl nods.

"Oh, I do need help, sweetheart." The disgusting perv licks his lips and lets go of the girl, prowling toward me.

I'm made to seduce men, but I can also scare the crap out of them and break their noses when the situation demands it. My fist splits his face in two before I can form a thought, and I shake out my hand, jolts of pain radiating across my knuckles. The bastard had strong bones.

With a gasp, the girl covers her face with her hands.

"What the fuck?" He gurgles, and blood sprays everywhere.

Gripping his greasy hair, I angle his ear to my mouth. "You'll leave that girl alone. You'll go home, shave your disgusting beard, and reflect on how you became such a loser." The compulsion dilates his pupils. Humans are so easy to manipulate.

He bolts off without a word, and I eye my damsel in distress with suspicion. I've run into situations like these where the girl gave me hell for saving her ass. *Love* is a funny thing.

"Thank you." She tucks a strand of hair behind her ear, her cheeks red.

I dust off my jacket and hook it around my elbow. "You're welcome."

"How did you—"

"Krav Maga. Google it." I glance at her name tag. "He won't bother you anymore if you don't go looking for him. Older guys are sexy, I get it, but he's sleazy." Our gazes lock, and I crank up my powers. The demonic haze ought to make a lasting impression on her. "Stay away from creeps, Heather." I stomp off, satisfied by my good deed.

FIGHTER

VICKY

My journey to California takes me deep into the heart of Middle America, and I spend a few days under the Texan sun, sampling sexy cowboys. My last stop is Arizona where a few friends of mine have set up shop.

Two vandellas I've known for years own a fusion cuisine place in Phoenix, and they're the exact company I need right now: fun and uncomplicated. Our powers don't work on each other, so I can actually relax in the presence of my own kind and know they're not secretly chatting with me so I'll fuck them later.

As soon as I step into Isabel's restaurant, my stomach lurches. The homey atmosphere has been replaced by a smothering silence. Nobody is chatting at the tables or raising their glasses in cheer, the place emptier than my ex-husband's heart. The red curtains are closed, and the feeble sunshine filtering through the sheer fabric twinkles against airborne lint particles.

"Isabel?" I call out, the hairs on the nape of my neck rising in time with the puffs of dust under my feet. I'm clearly the first customer to come through the doors in weeks.

"Vicky?" Isabel's voice is quiet, a stark contrast to her usual joyful tone. She appears from the revolving kitchen door and stops when she sees me. Her long black hair is tied in an untidy bun behind her head, her red-rimmed eyes wet with unshed tears.

I step closer to my friend. "What's going on?"

Her gaze darts to the floor. "It's Cora. She's missing." Cora's her twin sister, and they are inseparable.

"Oh, no! How long—"

She sniffles. "Three weeks."

I'm not sure that the twins have spent more than half a day apart since they were born, and my throat tightens. "Do you know who did it?"

"I have an idea..." She fumbles in her jacket's pocket for a tissue and presses a few buttons on her cell.

I squeeze her shoulder. "I'll help you get her back."

"Thank you. Tea?"

"Sure." She ushers me into her adjoined apartment behind the kitchen and motions for me to sit at one of the white textured chairs by the glossy quartz island. The electric kettle wheezes as she plugs it into the outlet. A few spoonful of Oolong Tea are dumped in a terra-cotta teapot. Isabel is still crying, sniffling into a Kleenex, and I give her some time to breathe.

We wait a few minutes for the tea to infuse, and she serves us both a cup.

I blow on the steaming beverage. "Tell me everything. Was it one of her regulars? Was it a demon?" Vandellas are sought-after mates, and it's not that unusual for a lovelorn ex or a jealous lover to try to enslave us into submission. Mind-blowing sex and craziness often go together. "I know people. They could do a spell and locate Cora quickly if you gave me some of your blood. You are identical twins, so your blood has got to be the same as hers, right?"

Isabel turns green, and her hands shake. "Listen, Vicky... it wasn't a regular. It was vampires..."

A loud engine roars onto the street in front of the restaurant.

My friend plays nervously with her necklace. "I'm so sorry."

A flurry of muffled footsteps echoes in my sensitive ears, and my blood turns to ice in my veins. Vampires... as in the creatures that have been hunting me. "You sold me out." An anchor of disappointment sinks in my chest, dragging down the last shred of trust I nurtured toward the universal laws of friendship and decency.

A loud cry dribbles from Isabel's guilty lips. "It's not just Cora. They've been raiding every vandella-owned establishment looking for you. They took one girl from each family and vowed to keep them hostage until you were surrendered to them. V, I'm so, so sorry."

"Not sorry enough, clearly," I say, kicking off my beautiful, peep-toe Valentino pumps.

I do the only thing a demon can do in this situation. I run. For a five-foot-four woman, I'm a hell of a runner. I slam the back door open, the tall apartment buildings towering from above. The trash and recycling bins clank together as I bump them with my elbow.

The smell of rotten fish clogs my nose. Two leather-clad, male vamps are blocking the exits on each side of the alley, and I stop. My bare feet dig into the gravel. A fire-escape ladder hangs from a balcony about twelve feet above me, and I jump with my hands stretched above my head. A proud grin curls my lips as my knuckles turn white against the base of the ladder, and I scurry upwards. The rusty bars are slippery as fuck, a thin film of rain from this morning's storm still licking the metal.

The vampires follow, their weight pulling the ladder down.

I kick the one directly below me in the forehead, and he grunts when his back collides with the ground. The second one stays out of reach, and I climb until I'm at the top of the building, my lungs and knees hurting.

The roof is square and barren. I run to the opposite edge and peer over it. Vampires patrol the street in front of the restaurant, holding a few passersby at bay, their fake police cars the perfect explanation for this manhunt. My chest heaves. I count eight bloodsuckers in total and scan their bare arms for the Delacroix's mark, but none of them seems to bear the tattoo. They probably belong to another family. I bet Ludovic called in a few favors to see me home quickly.

The closest building is a stretch too far, but it's the only possible escape. If I manage to jump on the neighbor's roof, I'll have a clear way down the street and might be able to disappear into the crowded boulevard. The first vampire spills onto the roof from the way I came.

I crouch, my toes planted firmly in the ground, and consider the height of the ledge. I'll have to pick up speed, use the ledge as a stepping stone, and jump. There's no time to aim for anything particular; I'll just hope for the best.

I leap into action, pushing myself, and dive feet first from the tall roof. I hang in midair for a moment, my gaze searching for a safe place to land, but the ground is coming way too fast, and the building is still too far away. A bad whiplash slices through my neck as my fingers finally grasp a railing, my head flying backwards. Dangling off the neighbor's alcove windowsill, I grit my teeth. My muscles scream from the abuse, and I need a moment to recover from my bad jump.

A vampire is perched on the balcony two stories below me.

He was bitten young, at sixteen or seventeen, and he's handsome, his spiky hair perfectly gelled. A loud grunt escapes him, and he flings himself a story higher, his long arms now barely six feet away from my ankles.

He shoots me an impressed smile. "I didn't think you'd make that jump."

"You and me both, Twilight." I exhale and start climbing, heading for the nearest balcony. A cold hand closes around my leg, and the weight of my pursuer stops my ascension. Twilight crawls over me like a vine. Damn vampire stamina. His arm encircles my waist, and I let go, hanging from his grasp like a very annoyed Barbie doll. Two others come to his aid, climbing the wall. Their black arms and legs remind me of spiders scurrying up their nets to collect their bounty.

The three vamps slowly lower me to the ground, passing me around as though we're *Cirque du Soleil* acrobats. I scratch one eye, kick one pair of balls and bite a neck on my way down, but it doesn't seem to bother them enough to drop me. There's now about a dozen vamps in police uniforms waiting below, and I know I've lost this round.

Once my feet hit the asphalt, they tie my hands behind my back with zip ties. Twilight presses hard on my jaw and forces a red liquid down my throat. The jasmine taste is unmistakable, so I know it's a sleep potion. He snaps a picture of me with his phone before they throw me in the back of a huge armored, red-striped SUV.

Pɪɴᴋɪsʜ ᴄʟᴏᴜᴅs sᴛʀᴇᴛᴄʜ towards a deep blue sky when I wake up in the back seat of a moving car. I'm lying down on the leather, my head bumping against the door every few seconds. The scenery blurs beyond the windows, the highway flanked by high trees. Twilight is typing on his phone at my feet, and the driver is arguing over who gets to choose the music with the vamp sitting next to him.

A smirk glazes my lips.

Three vampires and a conscious vandella locked in a car... They clearly haven't dealt with my kind before. I'm baffled that they didn't fly me over to Europe immediately. Maybe they wanted to set up some kind of exchange. Moving slowly, I test the strength of my restraints, but they're pretty solid. Bummer.

The movement catches Twilight's attention, and I bat my eyelashes at him. "Nice moves out there."

He braces his hands against the back of his neck, his arms stretched on each side, his muscles bulging inside his leather jacket. My short, black dress is hiked up almost to my waist, and I catch him stealing a glance at my lace panties. *Piece of cake.*

I slide my bare foot up his thigh, and he sucks in air. "You know what I am, don't you?" I drawl, whipping my powers up into a frenzied wave and letting it wash over him. His length hardens immediately beneath my toes.

"Yes," he breathes.

"If you let me go, I'll be very grateful."

The front passenger cranes his neck around. "Don't chat with her. Give her another dose."

My prey fumbles with his jacket's inside pockets. I press on his crotch. He drops a small vial that bounces off his knee and disappears beneath the driver seat. Instead of reaching for the potion, Twilight leans closer, lust dilating his pupils and making his red eyes a shade warmer.

"You want to kiss me, don't you?" I sit and stretch toward him. "It's better than you can imagine."

"Stop, Ian! *Stop right now,*" the driver screams.

Ian moans as I glide my tongue across his bottom lip, and just like that, I've won. *Thank you very much.*

I drink his energy in, ravaging his mouth and recharging my batteries. "Untie me, Twilight."

He frees me, spellbound. I discard the zip tie, elbow him right in the nose and snap his neck. That won't kill him, but it'll buy me time. I can't quite behead him with my bare fingers.

The car swerves, and the other two try to get a hold of me, their arms clawing at emptiness. One finger hooks itself in the fabric of my dress, ripping a few buttons open. They both freeze. My breasts are a killer asset. The passenger is too busy ogling them to prevent me from punching him square in the nose. He cries out in pain, his hands flying to his damaged bones.

I wrap my arm around the driver's neck from behind. "Pull over."

His hands clench around the steering wheel. "No."

I hop in his lap and try to push down the brakes.

The car flies off the road, our bodies hanging in mid-air for a moment before we all tumble around the cabin. My skull cracks the windshield, a humongous headache slicing through me. The screech of metal booms through my ears, and we land upside-down in the ditch.

Dizzy, I pat my head, my fingers digging into a mess of tangled locks. Glass shards bite into my ass as I sit up. The driver's got a huge piece of sunroof embedded in his neck, a red wave gushing from the wound. He shuffles around, and a sharp pain thunders inside my stomach. I let out a strangled shriek and look down.

The fucker impaled me on a silver dirk. I yank it out of me and slice his head off. His body explodes in a cloud of dust, leaving only a clump of clothes behind, and I cough his acidic leftovers out of my lungs. The passenger's head was bashed in by the glove compartment, but I cut his throat, too. Good beheading techniques are key to a worry-free life.

Twilight is nowhere to be found. He might have been ejected through a window or dusted by the accident. I exhale, pushing the stinging pain to the corners of my mind. Ashes soil my hand when I pat down the driver's clothes for a phone. A victorious grunt escapes me when I grip my stolen cell, but a weird crackling sound prevents me from dialing.

A loud boom at the front of the car is followed by an orange flash of light visible through the windshield. The smell of melting wires pervades the air, and I crawl out as fast as I can through a broken window, the engine fire heating up my arms.

Tall pines dance before my woozy vision when I finally manage to stand, the trees knitted so close together that they blur into a green and brown blotch. Hands shaking, I press on my belly and dial Liam's number. Calling my ex for help was *so* not on my list of things to do today, but shit happens. Lately, shit happens to me a lot more than it happens to other people.

My brows furrow at the absence of the ringing sound. No reception. Great.

Black smoke burns my lungs, so I walk away from the fire. Flames are slowly creeping toward the console, and with my luck, the whole thing is going to explode soon.

The chill of the night bites into my feverish skin. My bloody fingers cramp around the surviving buttons of my dress as I pop them into place. When I'm half-decent, half-roadkill, I slump to my butt in the squishy leaves littering the bottom of the trench.

The slope leading back to the road is too steep for my stab wound, and I wait for the sound of passing cars to keep me company and give me hope. Maybe someone will see the fire and rescue me. My lure sparks, creating a glitchy glimmer over my skin. The demonic survival-mode is kicking in. I could really use a kiss right now to boost my healing abilities, but there's no warm body available. Nothing but suffocating flames dancing to an ominous cricket choir.

The moon rises high in the sky, but there's still no cars. No knight in shining armor to respond to my lust beacon and feed me his energy —and his lips. Shadows lurk at the edge of my vision. I'm either going to bleed out, or I'll survive the wounds only to succumb to hunger in the middle of the woods.

Ain't that a stupid way to die.

EXTRAORDINARY GIRL

DOMINIC

*T*he leaves crunch under my paws as I run at full speed through the luscious woods. Pine. Oak. Freedom. A skinny squirrel runs up a tree. His fear seeps through the air and awakens my predatory senses, but I need much more than a fancy rat to quench my hunger.

The moon is at its peak. I should turn back, having already passed the west border, but I love to run.

I come to a screeching halt when a completely new and alluring scent barrels into my snout. I sniff the air once. Twice. *Wow.* Cookies and champagne. Each burst of speed brings me closer to the source, the smell even more powerful now. My claws dig into the soft earth of the trails next to the regional road. Gabe will have my head for coming so close to human civilization, but it's the middle of the night.

The wind guides me to my goal, and I distinguish other scents: gasoline, roasted metal and melted tires. The trees grow scarce near the edge of the forest. A car is upside-down deep in the trench separating the woods from the road. The engine emits tiny crackles and whirls of smoke, and I search the debris, snout to the ground, heading down the steep slope.

Coffee. Chocolate. Bubble gum.

Sweat. Fear. Blood.

A girl.

She looks to be in her early twenties. A torn black dress hangs off her frame, and her white skin glows under the moonlight. She's lying on the bed of leaves matted with fresh blood. There's no noise, not one human or inhuman heartbeat within a mile radius except hers and mine, so I prance over to her.

Why would this girl possess such a maddening scent? Now that I'm close, I can practically taste it on my tongue. Sugar and spice make my mouth water, a high feat considering my wolf prefers raw flesh. Despite the blood soaking her dress, her heart is beating steadily, and she doesn't look in pain, her features serene.

The eerie pull grows stronger, my control evaporating by the second, the need to touch her overwhelming, but I resist the urge to lick her neck. All bets are off when my wolf tastes human blood. Instead, I concentrate hard on my breathing, willing the change to come forth. My bones crack and snap as they rearrange themselves, and I stand up. Wet, half-decomposed leaves stick to my knees.

A huge black wolf erupts from the woods behind me. Gabriel's ears are raised in alarm, and his fur is sticking in all directions the way it does when he's annoyed. A change in the breeze tells me Sam isn't far behind, his scent getting stronger by the second.

I meet my alpha's gray stare. "It's a girl. There's a lot of blood, but she's alive."

Gabriel sniffs the air above the body.

"She smells *sooo* good, doesn't she? Sweet and... cinnamon-y."

He morphs into his human form and considers my discovery with dark eyes and a clenched jaw. "She smells like trouble."

Sam walks out of the bushes, his chestnut curls flying in the wind. "Still. We should help her."

I kneel next to the girl and graze her cheek. "She's a bit cold."

"Like a vamp?" Gabriel asks, his teeth bared.

Sam presses two fingers to her pulse point. "Like hypothermia."

Gabe crosses his arms. "There's a weird aftertaste of rotten blood-sucker in the air—what are you doing?"

I cradle her in my arms, carrying her bridal-style. "She weighs nothing."

Sam pinches her skin and brushes her lip. "She's dehydrated."

"Why did you pick her up?" Gabe growls.

"We're not going to leave her here, are we?"

The alpha shrugs. "We don't know her."

Ever since Evelyn left, Gabriel is wary of strangers. I get it.

"We have to help." Sam gives Gabe a pointed glare. "Let's get her warm first; we can argue after."

We're miles from the house, so I tread forward with long strides. There's something fascinating about her. I can't quite put my finger on what and school my gaze back on the trail, but my treacherous eyes keep darting back to the girl. I'm lucky I have superhuman reflexes, or I'd trip over every branch while I admire her.

Blond strands of hair waft in the wind, brushing my arm, and I press her cold body closer to my hot skin. Her eyelashes sparkle like glitter. Small sighs flow through her blue, heart-shaped lips, and full breasts strain against her black buttoned-up dress.

She's heating up under my touch.

Suddenly, an undiluted wave of fresh, hot desire squeezes my guts.

"Guys, something weird is happening." I press my lips together when another storm unfurls. There's a certain part of my anatomy that's suddenly very interested in my cargo.

Sam's voice booms from my right. "Dom! Are you seriously hard right now? She's covered in blood and unconscious."

I grit my teeth. "I don't know why." I'm usually not lusting after beaten-up strangers I find in the woods. Even the eerily beautiful ones. I walk another few minutes before my dick twitches painfully.

Lust radiates up my spine, and I groan. "Okay. Something is definitely not right."

I dump her into Sam's arms. A deep shudder rocks my body, and a few minutes tick by before I can breathe steadily again. I drag behind Sam and Gabe, my shoulders hunched, appalled by what happened.

A few miles down the path, it's Sam's turn to moan. "Oh, hell. What is that?"

If Sam has a hard-on for the girl, then I'm definitely not to blame. My heart starts beating faster. "Right?"

Gabe shakes his head. "You boys are just sad."

The corners of my mouth quirks up. "Pass her to Gabe. He hasn't had a boner in years."

Sam presses his lips together not to laugh, and I end up on my stomach biting the dirt.

"Fuck you, Dom." But he takes the girl into his arms.

We jog the last mile, and I can't help but peek to see if Gabe is immune to whatever is going on. He's not, but he seems to be handling it better. He notices me checking his junk and growls.

We finally make it to the cabin and deposit our precious visitor on Sam's surgery table.

"Get a catheter kit. I'll check her injuries and hook her up to warm fluids," Sam says as he puts on a pair of pants and his white doctor coat.

I never get why he wears white to examine bloody patients. Doing his laundry is a nightmare. Ugh. Talk about an impractical, nonsensical color scheme.

I rummage through the cabinet behind me until I find what he's asking for and pass the right Tupperware to him. Sam cuts the fabric of her dress at the belly button and gently peels it up her stomach to examine the source of the bleeding. The red clots are matted with dried leaves and pine needles.

Fresh scars run across her abdomen, and my fingers twitch at my sides.

Who could do something like this? And on our turf? The white-hot anger boils my blood, and I sit next to her on a stool, the urge to save her, to protect her getting stronger by the second. "Is she going to be okay?"

Sam starts cleaning the wound with gauzes soaked in saline. "I have no idea."

"Why did we react like that?" I wave in the general direction of my crotch.

"No idea," Sam clips.

"It's magic, right? I mean—it's got to be some sort of spell?" I ask, peering to see if the injury is serious.

He scowls like I'm an obnoxious toddler and flips on the surgical lighting. The bright spots imprint themselves in my retinas.

I swivel from side to side, feeling fucking helpless. Her face is half covered by a knot of blond hair, and I brush it behind her ear. "She's so beautiful."

Gabe yanks me upwards by the arm with an abrupt shove. "Come. Sam will clean her up while we double back to find clues about her attacker or her identity."

My mouth opens in outrage. "Sam can stay with her, but I can't?"

"I trust Sam. He's not a creep like you," Gabe says with a wolfish grin.

SOMETHING HUMAN

SAM

The lost girl looks so small on the exam table that is mostly used to stitch big, burly werewolves. I wet a clean towel and squeeze the excess of warm water out.

Very few buttons of her black dress have survived the accident and the walk over here, so I tug on the curtains and cover the big floor to ceiling windows of my surgical suite. DeLuca might come around if he smells something unusual, being his dependable noisy self, and I don't want anyone else in the pack to know about our guest yet.

I gently pry open one eyelid and shine a bright light into her eye. Both pupils contract, so her reflexes are intact. Her irises are dark and almost... purple. I school my mind into physician mode, inspecting her body now that I've gotten rid of the blood clots. She's been stabbed recently, and I trace the shape of the wound, testing the margins. They are already secured, and yet there's not contraction or signs of inflammation. It's not so different from the way we heal, and it's definitely supernatural.

It confirms my hunch that she's not human.

I draw some blood and sniff the vial. A big frown wrinkles my nose. The scent is exceptionally sweet. Mouth-watering, really, and I have never craved human blood.

But again, she's not human.

While the machine analyzes the sample, I continue my exam. Besides the scars on her abdomen, she's perfect. Literally. Her muscles are more developed than what you'd expect from a girl who possesses such a figure. I hold her ankle with care and pry a shard of glass from her bare foot. A weird warmth buzzes through my fingers.

Her results pop up on my computer's screen with a small beep.

She's got a mild regenerative anemia, so her bone marrow is already reacting to the blood loss, giving me yet another clue that she heals faster than she should. I hook her up to warm fluids and recheck the stab wound for signs of internal bleeding. I push down on her abdomen, but there's no swelling or tightness. The capillary refill time is good, and she's already not as pale as she was when we found her. There's no contusion on her head, but my fingers get tangled up in her hair. The silky strands seem to shimmer with their own light. It's like they're... pulling me closer.

My other hand travels up her arm until her pulse thuds beneath my fingertips. It's stronger than before. Gritting my teeth, I hide my face in the crook of her neck and inhale. God, she smells like my favorite upside-down cake.

I jolt backwards, my face searing in shame. *Did you just smell your patient? What the hell?*

A deep breath heaves her chest, and her features tense.

"Hey, can you hear me?" I ask.

"Hungry," she whispers, her voice and lips cracking.

I put a kettle on and whip up some chicken broth before pouring the mix it in a mug. Steam rises from the soup. I blow on it and steal a sip to make sure it's not burning hot.

After hiking her head up with a pillow, I offer her a spoonful, but she's limp and unconscious again. She's colder now, so I drape two large wool throws over her and heat a few bean bags in the microwave. Once she's nestled in them, I grab Gabe's book of supernatural creatures, searching for one that fits the profile.

I flip page after page, but the closest thing I find to a drop-dead gorgeous woman with magical hair is a Gorgon. If she's one, dropping a few drops of blood into her mouth should make her demon teeth bulge. Hungry, she said. Hungry for blood, maybe? She's no vampire, but most demons drink blood.

Using a scalpel, I nick my index, hoping I'm wrong because gorgons are exceptionally violent.

I pry her mouth open. Maybe I should wait for the guys to come back, but my caution wavers in the face of my extraordinary patient. Her pulse is faint, sealing my resolve, and I let the blood drip into her mouth.

Of its own accord, my thumb grazes her blue lips, but my experiment doesn't bear any results. She's still so cold...

I clasp my hand over her freezing fingers. A spark of electricity tightens my skin into goosebumps, and a strange, smothering heat crawls up my spine.

She really is a sleeping beauty.

A deep breath causes her chest to push against the fabric of her dress, and the last button pops open.

I suck in air. The sight of her full, round breasts squeezes my guts into knots and creates a tent situation in my scrubs. I screw my eyes shut, but somehow all my normal ethics and gentlemanly manners have deserted me. Like it's being reeled in by an undeniable force field, my hand inches closer and closer to that damn perfect pebbled peak until—

"Stop." Gabe's voice overrides whatever spell has been cast on me, and I back away, stunned by my behavior and unforgivable lack of self-control.

Gabe ushers me away from my patient, and my shoulders slump in shame. "God have mercy. I don't know what came over me."

He pats my back. "Don't beat yourself up. Something is clearly going on here."

My fists curl, and I walk away from the girl.

Dom takes in the beauty before him, and his eyes widen. My first instinct is to drag him away. It makes absolutely no sense, but I feel territorial of her.

Gabe catches my aborted movement. "No one touches the girl for now. I'll do some research."

ARABELLA

DOMINIC

"*T*here was a definite vamp dust smell hidden underneath hers," Gabe announces after he whisks us out of the exam room.

Sam stiffens.

Vampires and wolves never get along. Something about fire and ice. We run hot. They run cold. We're perfect enemies.

I sink my nails into my neck, trying to forget the sight of the girl's full breasts. Their shape. How perfectly they'd fit into my hands... "I called Billie, and she hasn't given out speeding tickets on this road in ages, but she'll patrol tonight in case someone searches for the van. DeLuca can tow it in the morning."

Sam's fists are curled at his side, his body rigid, and his ears are a flaming shade of red.

I grin. "What about you Sam? Or were you too busy copping a feel to examine her?"

Gabriel kicks me in the shins.

"She's definitely not human. Her blood marrow is already replacing the red cells she lost, and her skin is almost good as new," Sam says.

"What is she?" I ask.

He traces the arch of his brow. "I don't know."

We both turn to Gabe. Our alpha shakes his head, his nose wrinkled in the pout that has been stuck on his face for the better part of the last decade. "Me neither."

I bring a hand to my chest. "My fate is shaken, boss. I thought you knew everything."

"I know *almost* everything." His cold glare makes my wolf squirm.

"Could she be a wraith?" I shiver at the thought.

"Wraiths aren't technically alive. This girl is healing fast, and her blood work is similar to humans," Sam says.

Knowing him, he probably went through the whole book of demons while we were outside.

My mouth dries up. "A shifter, then?"

Gabe snorts, "You wish."

I steal a glance into the exam room through the narrow window in the door. "Why would I wish that?"

He pinches my neck. "Because then that little fantasy I see forming in your Neanderthal brain might come to pass."

"Is there someone we could call?" Sam proposes.

Gabe plucks his jacket from the back of the kitchen chair and swings it over his shoulders. "I'll visit Rickard, and you two will go to bed." He locks the door to Sam's world and hurries to the front of the house. Right before stepping over the threshold, he pauses, and his stare zeroes in on me. "If I catch you in there, you'll be in big trouble. Am I making myself clear?"

"Crystal, boss." I salute him with a laugh and head off to my room.

Sam follows. "Can I borrow Gabriel's copy of the demonologist? He said he lent it to you."

"Sure." I rummage through my desk and get it for him. I was

supposed to study that book, but the cover is dusty, and the page marker is tucked halfway through chapter one.

Sam leaves with the thick volume, and I spin my computer chair from one side to the other, unsure of what to do.

I rap my fingers against my laptop and Google "sexy demon." Bad idea all around. I'm met with images that don't do my girl justice, but also a word that sets my imagination on fire. Succubus.

I snap the screen shut and jump into bed. The sheets are tangled at my feet, but I don't bother with them. I'm hot enough as it is thinking about sex demons and the like. My palms are sweaty, and the bulge in my pants is getting impossible to ignore.

Hours tick by without a whiff of sleep.

I slip out of bed and sneak into the kitchen, avoiding the creaky floorboards as I move across the living room. Sam is probably still reading. Gabe thinks I don't know where he keeps the master key, but he's wrong. The doorknob clicks when I open the lock, and I wait a few seconds before inching the door open.

God. She's exactly as we left her. Immobile. Beautiful. Magnetic.

I drag my knuckles against her cheek.

She's freezing, and before I can stop myself, I throw my shirt over my head and climb next to her. I don't care what Sam and Gabe say. Skin to skin is still the fastest way to heat up a body. A supple, feminine one at that. I volunteer happily.

Shit. My thoughts are going down the gutter faster than torrential rain. I flatten my palm to her cold stomach and examine the stab wound. It's barely visible now, and my throat eases an inch. The bag of fluids is half empty, but she's colder by the second. Acid scratches my throat.

Why isn't she waking up?

I stroke her arms, telling myself I'm doing it to warm her up. The light catches a shimmering pattern beneath her skin, and I press my nose against her shoulder. Her scent is divine, like a hot steaming cup of Chai. I dart my tongue out. She tastes like my favorite desert sushi topped with the most expensive sparkling French wine. With a groan, I nibble her neck. Her jugular is exposed, and the predator in me shudders.

A pretty pink color returns to her lips, chasing away the purplish-blue hue, and I can't help but stare at their sensual shape. My thumb grazes her mouth, my erection returning to its earlier peak faster than a space rocket heading for the moon.

I snort, thinking she's like Snow White. A princess found in the woods, and if I kiss her, she might wake up. I grin at my own childishness, but her lips are becoming redder and redder, and I lick mine in anticipation.

As if possessed by some invisible ghost, I lean in and press my mouth to hers.

SWEET DREAMS

VICKY

The haze of death lifts, and I jolt awake, a pair of hot lips pressed against mine.

My head throbs, my muscles ache, and my breaths are painful and shallow, but all of that barely registers against the red-hot need that sets my nerves ablaze.

I'm. So. Hungry.

The powerful body next to me stiffens, but I arch into my savior, the heat of his naked chest delicious against my cold, starving skin. I blink, thankful for the darkness, my eyes hurting from the feeble glow coming from a laptop screen on the other side of the room. I'm lying on a stainless steel table, the metal cool underneath my palms. This isn't the morgue, right? Because... gross!

There are no refrigerators or autopsy instruments lying around. *Phew.* The desk propped against the wall is cluttered with papers and books, a sofa sagging in the corner.

The man shifts. "Fuck. It worked." He has black hair that's longer on top and shorter on the sides, tanned skin, and clear hazel eyes. He's young. Twenty, maybe? Better yet: he's not a vampire. I run my fingers over his chiseled face, the angular jawline and proud nose making my heart throb.

His dark stubble prickles my skin, and I catch his scent. He's a wolf. *Yum.*

"I'm so sorry for kissing you... I mean—"

I lick his neck, the thin film of sweat filling my mouth with saliva.

He caresses the back of my ear with a husky groan, his thumb tracing the shape of my lips. "Who are you?"

"No talking." I grab a fist of dark hair and tug him back down to my mouth. With shaky hands, I follow the shape of his strong shoulders, my knees and arms weak from the hunger. He deepens the kiss. A silky tongue dances against mine, his woodchip-and-campfire smell going straight to the space between my legs.

I need everything he has to offer, and I need it now. I wiggle against him. "Please."

He peels himself off me, and I realize he thought I was pushing him away.

"No. Come back. I need you," I whimper, my throat painful and stiff.

His hand twitches against my thigh, and I spread my legs as an invitation, unable to say another word.

Black spots dance before my eyes. I know I barely have seconds before I faint again. If I pass out, he probably won't fuck me, and I'll die.

A taller man with kind eyes wearing a white coat thunders into the room, his mouth opening in shock. "*Dom!* Stop!" He rips my wolf off me, and I could cry from the loss, but darkness claims me again.

PRECIOUS

SAM

Good thing I needed a glass of water, or Dom would have raped my patient. I'm holding him in a rear choke hold, ready to knock him unconscious if needed. He's young and impetuous, but with wolves, age and rank trump hot-blooded and reckless.

"She asked for it," he says, struggling to break free.

I smack his shoulder hard and let him go. "She was barely conscious."

"I think she needs it."

I shake my head. "You've gone insane, man."

"Touch her." He clutches my hand and presses it against the girl's stomach.

It's hot. Not warm. Hot. Like black rocks under the desert sun, and the heat seeps into my cells, tingling across my skin, my chest, and my... I squeeze my eyes shut, my breathing ragged. "What the hell is that?"

"I told you so." He wraps a hand around her limp arm, watching her closely.

I snatch my book from the table. "Did you see her eyes clearly?"

Dominic paces the room back and forth. "How can you be thinking about her eyes right now? Don't you smell her?"

He's talking about the powerful and delicious scent of arousal coming from between her legs. "Of course I do, genius." I smack his head. "Still, Gabe said—"

He comes to an abrupt stop in front of me. "I don't give a fuck what Gabe said. I kissed her and she woke up. She blacked out again only when you separated us. I know what I felt."

My scientist brain is always ready for an experiment. "Okay. Let's say I believe you. She should wake up again if you touch her."

"Maybe."

I cross my arms over my chest, ready to give this a try.

Dom cups her cheek and watches her face like she's the corpse of a brown bear he just killed.

"Don't eat my patient." I swat his hand away and flatten my palm to her neck.

"I'd never eat her—" A fierce blush spreads on his cheeks.

"—you know how you get when—"

He swallows a growl. "How many years will you hold that over me?"

I shoot him a unimpressed glance, my touch having no effect whatsoever on the girl.

He scratches the back of his neck. "I had to kiss her before."

"Fine."

He crushes his lips to hers. His passion, determination, and total disregard for caution always baffles me. I'm about to intervene when she stirs and kisses him back.

"I'll be damned." I fall to my ass on the chair next to my desk.

They make out like they want to breathe each other in, Dom's moans making it clear how much he's enjoying himself. A golden glow flickers over the girl's skin as they grind against one another, and

Dom's theory no longer sounds so crazy. Maybe she's feeding on his touch.

She blinks once, twice, her long eyelashes mesmerizing. Her gaze jumps from Dom to me, and she hooks her small hand around his neck. "I'm almost too weak to feed anymore. One of you is going to have to drop his trousers soon."

Dom and I exchange a look, his eyes burning with pride because he was right. I jump to my feet, but Dom starts peeling off his jeans, eager to follow her instructions.

Our gazes lock, and her deep purple irises freeze me in place. The ruffle of fabric fills the room. It's like she's staring into my soul, her intense beauty awakening something deep and deserted inside my soul, and I can't look away.

She is still staring at me when Dom descends upon her stark naked.

"You plan to watch?" She asks, her voice gruff.

I pass a hand over my heated face, breaking the spell. "Right. Sorry."

A hot weight presses on my chest, and I slam the door behind me.

The living room is silent except for the light breeze whistling inside the screened porch door. The flat, consistent buzzing of the refrigerator slowly coaxes me back to reality, and I put on a pot of coffee.

My hands twitch over the mug handle when a long, enraptured scream pierces my bubble, coming from *my* office.

A stinging wave of jealousy unfurls in my bones. They just met. Literally.

How can they have sex so quickly? Most importantly—Why does it bother me?

Rolling my eyes, I sip on the steaming beverage, the bitter tang of black coffee uncoiling my dark thoughts. It's been so long since I kissed a woman... maybe the sting of loneliness is coming back to haunt me. Maybe her powers are to blame for the weird feeling cramping my chest. Maybe it's natural for me to wonder what would have happened if she'd chosen me...

I'm the doctor. I should have connected the dots.

How hypocritical of me to both judge and envy them... It's not their fault if my heart is broken beyond repair.

BLANK SPACE

VICKY

*T*he handsome doctor with short chestnut curls heads out the door, and my stomach squeezes with regret. "Why did he leave so quickly? I meant he should join."

The sexy dark-haired stranger hovering above me chokes on his breath. "God, you're serious."

My eyes rove over him, and my lips curl. He'll do just fine. I hiss and dig my nails into his sides. "Now!"

His length teases my entrance, but he holds back. "Wait! Should I get a condom?"

Supernatural creatures are immune to human diseases, and I can't have kids, so... "No!" My lure is coming off in big, uncontrolled waves, not responding to my commands. Survival instinct has kicked in, and there's no holding it back.

The pleasure on the wolf's face betrays a sharp edge of pain as he feeds me his cock inch by delicious inch. His eagerness allows me to see straight, the feel of him so fucking amazing after almost dying of hunger that I have to curl my fists not to hurt him.

We're both fighting to catch our breaths, but at least I'm not going to pass out again.

I caress the nape of his neck, enjoying the feel of his body pressing against me, pinning me down, stretching me out... "I'm Vicky."

"Dominic."

"Hey, Dominic." Running my fingers through his hair, I meet his shallow thrusts.

This would be awkward except it's not the first time this has happened to me, and it probably won't be the last. This is one of the fucked-up things I must deal with being what I am, and I've come to terms with the drawbacks and perks of my existence a long time ago. Hell, I'm hot for this tanned, rugged stranger. His touch is both hesitant and brash, an unlikely mix that sets my nerves ablaze.

"Could you help me with..." I motion to the scraps of black fabric left hanging around my body. They cling to my skin like scruffy fleece, and I sigh in relief when the wolf tears them off, most of the grime and dirt going with them.

He squeezes my sides, and I know he's dying for more. I trace the shape of his ear. "It's okay, Dominic. You can fuck me."

With a low, tortured howl, Dominic slams into me, swept away by the tsunami of lust I'm creating.

I cry out in approval. It's exactly what I need, but there's no denying that it's rough and messy. I feed off him shamelessly, swallowing every gulp of his desire.

The process quickly forces him over an edge he's not ready for, and I can tell from his pout—and the foul string of Italian curses—that he's upset by his performance.

His chest heaves, his breaths slowly returning to normal. "Whoa..." He staggers to his feet. His fingers skim my upper back before he picks me up in his arms and carries me to the couch in the corner of the room. The tower of books resting on one of the armrests is thrown off-balance, and the volumes scatter to the floor with faints thumps.

Dominic sits down with me on top.

I'm shaking, grateful for the gentle way he's holding me to his chest, my thighs on each side of him.

His breath flutters against my pulse point. "You feed on sex?"

I nod, enjoying the warmth of his skin. "Technically, I feed on the desire I incite in you."

"Wow."

I nip his earlobe. "Don't act so surprised. You feed on bunnies and deer, dear."

He whips his head back and stares deep into my eyes. "How do you know?"

"That you're a werewolf? Your scent." I drag my tongue across his neck. "Your taste." He smells like earth and fallen leaves, an all-male musk coating the nature tones, and I hum with joy.

"And what are you?" He breathes me in with fervor, too.

"A vandella."

He wraps a hand in my hair. "Not a succubus?"

"If I were a succubus, you'd be dead. Now that we've been introduced, kiss me."

He claims my mouth without question. His unrepentant tongue slides across mine, discovering every little groove like I'm the last well in the desert and he's dizzy with thirst. I grind my hips against his, reawakening his desire before it's time.

His lids flutter, his body going perfectly still. "Fuck. You pack a serious lusty punch."

"We could shout for your friend," I offer in earnest.

Pride flashes in his eyes. "I can go all night, baby."

I grin at his boastful outburst. He takes control even though I'm on top and lifts me all the way up only to bury himself deep again, muffling dirty praises against my neck.

The moisture between my legs makes it an easy glide, and my starved hands explore the planes of his chest. He's large and toned in every way that counts. His rich hazel eyes are hooded, and his fingers dig into my waist. Sweat and sex fill the air, our scents mixing together like crystallized sugar. No one can handle me in this state without losing a bit of themselves, but he seems to be enjoying the wild ride. A human would probably have fainted after that first round.

The merciless thrusts are like hot chocolate fudge, and the rush makes me heady. His abs strain at the furious rhythm. I lose track of how long it lasts, but it's longer than it should be. He's resisting his release.

I thought I was too famished to bother with an orgasm, so my mouth opens in shock when a swirl of pleasure surges in my belly, his hard shaft hitting just the right spot at just the right angle for my vision to blur and my legs to shake. An unbidden scream tears my throat, and my walls clench around him.

"Finally." His length throbs as he comes undone.

God, he's been waiting for me to come? He's seriously insane.

He rests his head back on the cushion, his breaths labored like he's forgotten how to exhale.

Wolves rarely wander into the city. I've been missing out on a very attractive and seriously robust gene pool.

My gaze wanders around the room. The exposed wood beams towering above us give the office a cozy vibe. Floor to ceiling windows are covered by thick curtains, and the rumble of computers and machines on the other side tickle my curiosity.

"Where are we?" I ask.

"This is Sam's exam room. You're in our house." Dominic pulls me flush against him. "I need... more."

I twist around to extricate myself from his grasp. "You've had enough. I can't control it, and I'm afraid it might kill you." I stand on wobbly legs.

"I don't care. I need it. I need..." Rough hands force me down to the floor, and I'm really turned on. His desperation is like a fine wine with caviar.

Despite my good intentions, I find myself on my knees, offering him the perfect angle, but his whole body is shaking with exhaustion.

God... I can't take the chance to kill my savior. I have to do something, but my nerves are begging me to surrender and enjoy the passion streaming from him. I flatten my body to ground.

"Help. Please! I don't want to hurt him." I yell as loudly as I can.

The door bursts open, and I meet the newcomer's stare head-on. Raw power oozes from his skin, and every single hair on my body rises to attention. An alpha. My mouth waters. I've never had one before.

He tears Dominic off me in one fluid motion. "Enough!"

YOU SHOOK ME ALL NIGHT LONG

DOMINIC

The sound of the shower running and a lovely rendition of Taylor's Swift Blank Space coax me out of my coma. I hop to my feet, my body aching from the barbaric sex I had last night. Despite my sore muscles, my flesh hums for more, and I follow the enticing voice of my siren.

The shower is made of glass, allowing me a wide but fogged view of her beauty.

She looks so different than yesterday. Her blond, almost translucent hair sticks to her neck, and her previously bluish skin is now the color of honey. A golden energy pulses around her while she sings her heart out, her mouth-watering body dancing along to imaginary music.

The spray of water hits me square in the neck when I pick her up in my arms. Her squeal of joy sends a direct jolt to my dick, and I hiss in pain.

She wraps her legs around my midriff. "I thought you'd sleep the day away."

"You roughed me up."

"Are you complaining?"

"Not in the least." Her red lips beckon, and I swallow her small talk into a furious kiss.

Feeling her melt against me, I angle her hips right and lower her down my length.

It's not like last night. She's dosing her powers, the lust not as hot and destructive as it was. It's fucking amazing, and I'm barely moving inside her. I lap water off her skin, drinking her in. My Snow White.

She sighs, and her nipples harden against my chest. Hell. I was too out of it to tend to her breasts last night, but they're magnificent. I lean in and take one pebbled peak into my mouth, her moans filling me with pride. She bucks her hips, and I grind against her. Hard. Deep.

Her body shudders. She screams as I ride her orgasm out, the process taking minutes instead of seconds.

When she scrapes bloody lines into my shoulder, I explode inside her. The release is both quick and slow, the pressure coiling in my shaft so acute that is almost hurts, but it's the best un-fucking-believable sensation I've ever felt.

"Damn, this is something else." I promise myself to build up my stamina so I can make it last longer next time.

Mouth opened, Vicky wipes the wet hair away from her forehead and struggles to catch her breath. "You're very dedicated."

I press my forehead against hers, still holding her weight. "My English teacher would disagree."

"Essays aren't quite the same thing as sex?"

"Not quite, though I'd gladly write one about you."

She throws her head back and laughs. The sound is clear and melodic, and as soon as it's over, I'm already plotting to hear it again. I envelop her in a soft towel and bring her back to my room, setting her down on my bed.

There's a tattoo on her hip bone, and my eyes narrow. "What's this?" She follows my gaze, and her fists clench. It doubles my curiosity, so I bend and look closer. "An ink splatter?" It's very delicate, the tattoo splashing across her skin like a real splatter would.

"Yep." She pulls on my arm, bringing me closer to her lips and away from the ink.

"What did you cover up with it? Your ex-boyfriend's name?" I joke, but her muscles turn to stone.

I fumble in my dresser and offer her a black t-shirt. The loose fabric falls above her knees, but it's low enough to be decent. The sight of her in my shirt sparks my lust anew. I snake a hand under the hem and grip her hip. "God, you're the most beautiful woman I've ever seen."

She trails her fingertips along the ridges of my abs. "You're not so bad yourself."

"Hum-hum." Gabe clears his throat loudly from the opened door. "Dom. A word."

I slip on a pair of jeans and follow him.

He ushers me to the kitchen. "Have you completely lost your marbles?"

"Why? Because I'm not second-guessing how I feel when I touch her? She's the most interesting thing that has happened to this town in the last decade."

Sam is standing by the island, typing on his laptop.

Gabriel blows past him on his way to the sink. "Interesting is another word for unpredictable."

"I've had enough predictability for one lifetime."

"May I remind you of what happened the last time your tempestuous self went rogue?" the alpha whispers angrily.

My shoulders sag. "No, boss."

Vicky joins us. She drags her fingers along the back of the couch, her eyes darting around our den. "This is quite a nice setup you have going on. Been here long?"

"Long enough to *own* it." Gabe's glower presses against the wolf part of my brain that's trained to seek his approval.

He's not talking about the house, or the land. He's talking about the woods, the mountains. The entire fucking town.

She struts over to Sam, my shirt barely covering her mid-thigh. "I'm Vicky. I'm a vandella."

"Not a succubus," I add.

"I'm Sam," he says, shaking her outstretched hand.

Gabriel punches the tap closed and drinks his water like it offended him by being too liquid or something.

Sam sits on the couch, clearly trying to downplay his height not to scare our guest.

"I'm really glad I passed out in your neck of the woods," Vicky jokes, her eyes meeting mine a second longer than it does Gabe's or Sam's.

I snatch two soda bottles from the fridge and offer her one. "I'm glad I found you."

Gabe's neck is stiff, his squared shoulders and curled fists intimidating as hell. "How long do you plan to stay?"

Sam's knuckles dig into the plush armrest at the clear dismissal, but the fucker refuses to meet my alarmed stare.

"Wait a minute—" One glare from Gabe kills the words before I form them.

Vicky's smile widens, but it has lost its warmth. It's the very definition of *icy.* "I'll be out of your hair pretty soon." She abandons her untouched Diet Coke on the table with a loud clank.

The front door closes behind her a second later.

I set my drink next to hers and run outside.

She's already whizzing up the road.

"Where are you going?" I shout at her back.

"Wherever." Her bare feet scratch against the gravel.

I almost whisk her up but fear it'll only fuel her anger. "You're a use-them-then-leave-them gal?"

Her shaky fists are braced against her hips, and she turns to face me. "I know when I'm not wanted. In fact, I'm fucking tired of being *unwanted.*"

The thought of anyone rejecting her is ludicrous, but behind her tight lips there's real sorrow, and I wonder where my goddess comes from. I'd kill to know her story, to unravel the mystery behind those broken purple irises. But I'm not good at romance, so I say, "Gabe's overprotective of us."

"He hates me."

"I don't hate you. Sam doesn't hate you. Gabriel is a sullen boring grown-up," I joke. "You should stay here with me. There's miles of wood and obnoxious shifters that way."

She cracks a smile.

I graze her cheek with my thumb. "Stay a few days. Maybe we can track the vamps that did this to you."

"They're dead. I dusted them."

"Still. Stay. I want to know more about the princess I found in the woods."

She slaps my chest playfully. "You're so corny."

"I've been called worse." I draw her in for a kiss. God, I can't get enough of her lips. Her scent. Her taste. She's barely been here for a day, and she owns me. Now, all I've got to do is convince Gabe to let me keep her.

DOCTOR JONES

VICKY

*D*ominic's warm body stirs against mine. We spent the rest of the morning chatting and kissing on his bed, away from the nasty stare of his alpha. The dude hates me for no reason at all, and I almost left merely because of the scary-aggressive vibe rolling off of him.

I trace lazy patterns over Dom's ripped stomach, letting a hint of lust trickle through my fingers.

He swats my hand away. "Not now. I have to go to work."

"You work?"

He jumps to his feet and pulls up his jeans. "Wolf work."

His skin his tanned and smooth, his abs flexing as he fumbles around the chaos in the room to find a clean shirt.

I grip the hem of denim and pull the fabric down his right butt cheek. "You have a minute."

He shackles my wrists with his hands and pushes me back on the bed. "I promised Gabe I wouldn't flake on my duties."

"In exchange for letting me stay?"

"Well... yeah," he says with a cute shrug.

I catch a pout from surfacing on my mouth. I hate complications. I don't *do* complicated, not when I'm not accidentally in love. *Which never happens.* "Off you go, then, little soldier." I smack his ass.

Mischief shines in his eyes. He's worth a few days of *complications.*

I take a long, hot bath in the big Jacuzzi those wolves clearly never use and make myself a sandwich in their modern kitchen.

This house is brand new, a few years old max. The smell of construction dust and fresh paint still lingers behind the wet wolf and hunky male musk, and I wonder where they lived before. Antsy for a distraction, I tiptoe into Sam's office.

The werewolf is sitting in front of a top-of-the-line row of three monitors, the screens displaying various medical reports. A large opened textbook is sprawled over his keyboard, and he's so focused on his reading that he doesn't notice my arrival.

His brows crease, his teeth biting down on a pencil. I've never found a yellow pencil so sexy before. Each toned muscle shaping his white coat has me wishing he'd draw on me instead of studying my blood work.

"Hello, doctor," I greet him huskily.

Maybe it's the white coat, but as Sam looks up at me from behind his monitors, I feel like he's the wisest of the three. I assumed Gabriel was the oldest because he's the alpha, but Sam's baby-blue eyes make me doubt my prior assessment.

I plop on the seat next to him. "I'm bored. Talk to me." I point to a graphic. "What's this?"

"This shows how many leukocytes of each type you have in your blood." His squared shoulders wiggle underneath the white coat.

"Leukocytes?"

"White blood cells," he breathes.

Who said science talk isn't hot? He's got a resting pretty-boy face, a large forehead and a chin dimple. His skin is smoother than mine despite my supernatural advantage. The clean-cut look isn't usually something that I'm attracted too. I prefer rough edges and a hint of danger, but I'm willing to make an exception. I rap my fingers delicately down his arm until I reach his bare wrist. He's got long, steady fingers. Doctor's hands. I brush his knuckles and tease him with a slight flare of lust, just enough to make him hard.

My powers spark off his skin, and he rips his hand away. "What about Dom? I thought you liked him."

I nudge him with my elbow. "I like him. I like you. The two aren't mutually exclusive."

He blinks and returns his attention to the damn book, his jaw clenched.

My pulse quickens. "How old are you?" He looks barely thirty, but wolves age very slowly after their first change. He might be a hundred for all I know.

He doesn't look up from his work. "It's rude to ask a wolf his age."

Wolves are known to be exceptionally loyal to their pack, and I brace my arms over my chest. "You're angry at me for coming on to you."

"I value loyalty."

"Loyalty and monogamy have nothing to do with one another. Not when there's no strict commitment between the parties. Dominic isn't a possessive man."

His eyes narrow. "How would you know?"

"I'm right, aren't I? He's the kind of man who's always up for an adventure. He likes to try new things, in life and in bed. And he's fearless."

Sam pushes the papers aside, angling his body to me. "That's an exceptionally accurate depiction of a man you just met."

"I have a special skill. I can taste someone's essence when I kiss them."

"I'll pass." He moves to stand but stops when I graze his arm.

Desire drips from him like sand through an hourglass. The heat of his skin radiates toward me, the slight dilation in his pupils leaving me no doubt that he's aroused. His gaze flicks to my lips.

"Come on. I know you're attracted to me."

"I'm intrigued by you, I'll admit," he says, his body awfully stiff.

I skip over to the couch to give him some space. Laying on my stomach, I prop my arms under a pillow. "Then ask me questions."

Sam finally relaxes in his chair. "How often do you have to feed?"

He's not talking about Chinese take-out. "Almost every day."

"And you feed on what exactly?"

I lick my lips. "Desire."

He huffs. "Desire? That's not concrete. You must be taking *something* in. A molecule."

I trace a random pattern on the cushion. "What if it's... magic."

Passion warms his face as he answers, "What you call magic, I call advanced science. I haven't seen real magic, yet."

"Then you haven't met the right girl." I punctuate my statement with a sexy tilt of the neck, my cleavage perfectly angled to make him sweat. I don't believe in soul mates, but I know what most people prefer to hear. A perfect someone... it's fantasy.

Sam opens and closes his mouth. "Do you have to touch your... meal?"

"Yes."

His gaze turns all analytical. "Then there's got to be something that passes between you and the man."

I grin. "It doesn't have to be a man."

And just like that, the doctor blushes.

He asks question after question, feasting on my mind instead of my body, and I must admit it's a nice change. I've never held a man so captive with my mouth before. Well... with my lips, yes, but not my words.

He takes notes. "Vandellas aren't in the book," he explains, his pencil flying across the paper.

"Planning to study the genus Vandella?"

"Imperfect references annoy me."

"Think that study might require a *close* examination of your subject?" I tease.

"Wow." He writes something down.

I prance over to him and read over his shoulder. He's got a few paragraphs already, and I skim the words. *Eerily beautiful. Gives off a type of lust-filled aura. Feeds on desire.* "Makes dirty uncle jokes?" I burst into a fit of laughter.

He presses his half-closed hand to his mouth. "Don't blame me. These results are accurate. One subject. One set of results. That's how bad studies are made." He's clearly struggling to keep a straight face.

"Now, my turn." I comb my fingers through his beautiful chestnut curls.

"I'd rather not." He angles his mouth away and pushes me gently aside, rising to his feet.

Blocking his escape, I lay my palm against his chest. His warmth seeps through the fabric, and my tongue scratches against the roof of my mouth. "It's not fair. I've answered all your questions. And you're dying to know if something will *pass* between us."

He shifts from one foot to the other.

A soft graze against the tender skin of my neck creates a ripple of need in my belly.

"Okay then. For the sake of your Sam encyclopedia." His eyes dart to my lips, then rise to meet my gaze before returning to my mouth. With a heavy sigh, he leans in, and he's tall enough that he has to really bend down. I stand on the tips of my toes, meeting him in the middle. His tongue drags across my bottom lip before he presses his soft lips to mine. It's barely a peck, and I find myself starving for more.

Sam is a man who doesn't like to be rushed. The energy he gives off is the exact opposite of Dominic's tempestuous and dauntless vibe. He's the calm before the storm. Warm. Solid. Not easily swayed. Musk and cologne caress my nose, his mouth-watering scent quickening my breath.

He pulls back before I can reciprocate, and I whimper at the loss. That definitely wasn't enough for me to feed on.

"So? What kind of man am I?" he asks softly.

"The good kind." I wink and strut away from my new favorite wolf. He's an old soul who prefers the hunt. The courtship. The seduction.

I'll let him chase me all he wants.

As I emerge into the kitchen, Gabriel's fists are clenched around the back of a chair, his dark eyes appraising my attire. Dom's shirt hangs loosely around my frame, the skewed neckline leaving one shoulder bare.

"Come with me. You need clothes, and if you're staying, you should know your way around town." His tone is flat, and yet Gabriel's deep voice and raw animal magnetism make it sound like one hell of an indecent proposal.

LIKE IT OR NOT

VICKY

The alpha drives a huge black pick-up truck. His dark hair, tanned skin and gray eyes give off a definite Mediterranean vibe, and I study the sinews and ridges of his impressive muscles. He could probably bench press three of me with one hand tied behind his back like Gaston does with the blond triplets.

"How many dozen eggs do you eat every morning?" I ask, giggling on the inside.

He looks at me like I'm crazy. "What?"

"Nothing. I'm rambling."

After ten minutes of thick woods, we emerge on a main road. At first, it looks like a typical B-movie rural small town. Hunting shop, grocer, barber. The smallest car is a compact SUV, big trucks roaring up and down the street. Some of them are modified and mounted on huge tires. Every single driver and pedestrian we cross paths with waves to Gabriel, and he waves back.

The butcher's storefront is particularly big, and I eye the old-style but freshly painted sign with curiosity. "What's this town called?"

"Wolf Creek." Gabriel's big hand grips the wheel like it personally insulted him.

"Very subtle," I say with a light chuckle, trying to defuse the tension, but something tells me my bad jokes won't charm Gabriel.

"We try." He parks in front of a large square building.

I jump to the ground, my bare feet scratching against the asphalt. The small parking lot is empty but for a blue-striped police car.

A woman holding a steaming cup of coffee stops abruptly in front of the truck. "Gabriel," she gasps.

The wolf slams his door shut and tilts his head in greeting. "Billie. Any news?"

"No, boss. I've been patrolling along the highway, and nothing is out of the ordinary." Her eyes are wide, and she looks me up and down like I'm famous or something.

Dom's t-shirt ends at my mid-thighs, and I'm guilty of a bad case of bed-hair. Very *teenage runaway*.

She leans in, but I'm not to blame because my powers are completely muted.

Gabriel is distracted, looking down at his phone, while Billie unmistakably sniffs the air around me.

"Hi. I'm Vicky." I extend my hand.

She hesitates but shakes it, her strong hold definitely wolfish. "You're Dominic's new girlfriend." It's not a question, confirming that I didn't imagine her scent-vestigation.

I grin. "Maybe."

"Billie's been checking the roads since you arrived. In case you were followed." Gabriel pats her shoulder with his huge hand. "Keep up the good work."

The woman blushes slightly and scampers off, but not before I spot a big goofy smile stretching her full lips.

I skip closer to Gabriel. "Billie has a crush on you."

"Don't be ridiculous. I've known her since she was a little girl," he grunts.

I roll my eyes. "Don't kill the messenger. She ain't a little girl no more, and she's hot for you."

He disappears into the building. It's one of those old general stores that sell a bit of everything. I thought places like these were extinct. In two strides, I go from the pharmacy section to the women's clothing aisle. Like a Macy's puked on a CVS at a party, and a Publix came to separate them. Definitely not *Dolce & Gabbana*, but my high maintenance days are as far behind me as my taste for monstrous men.

I unhook a checkered blouse and a denim skirt from the hangers and change. The lingerie selection is lacking, but I can pull-off the bra-less look.

The cashier's jaw falls to the floor, but Gabe steps in between us, blocking me from view.

A low growl rumbles at the back of the alpha's throat. "We have a visitor."

"I see that," the clerk croaks.

"She's welcome in town. For now." Gabriel cranes his neck around to glare at me as I tuck the last button in place.

"So, you guys are cowboys, then?" I place a large hat on my head.

"We need stock to survive," Gabriel says.

A wall of firearms glares at me from behind the cash register. One look into the clerk's eyes confirm my suspicion that he's also a wolf. What kind of shifter paradise did I end up in?

A pair of pretty leather boots catches my attention, and I snatch them from the rack. "I bet you all eat your meat rare."

"That's an easy bet."

I hop on the counter. "How many of you are there?"

The alpha nods to his subordinate, and the man disappears in the back.

"You ask too many questions." Gabriel's tone is icy and dangerous, and his hands clench around the edge of the glass counter-top.

My heart thumps, but I play it cool and cross my legs. The skirt hikes up my thighs. My experience with powerful, violent supernatural creatures tells me that honey has a better chance of bailing me out than claws. "You mind my questions?"

He knocks the boots to the ground. "I mind beautiful women smelling of vampires suddenly turning up in my town."

"You think I'm beautiful?" I lean forward, pushing my chest against the fabric of my new shirt.

His scent is salty and fresh. He puts one arm on each side of me, his broad frame caging me in.

A fiery tint flickers in his eyes. "I think you're a spy."

He exudes poise, but I'm not fooled. He's trying to force the truth out of me, and the pressure of his power is as vivid as a punch in the face. All creatures of the night have a certain talent for manipulating lesser minds, but I'm not a human nor an idiot, so his alpha-mojo is mostly useless against me.

"Are you a spy, Blondie?" His toes dig into the carpet, and between the stiff line of his jaw and the subtle twitch of his knuckles, he's ready to strike. He'll kill me in two seconds flat if I don't answer correctly.

This outing was a ruse to get me alone. I might not be a spy in the way he implies, but my true identity is a death sentence all the same. Somehow, I've stumbled upon the most organized wolf clan I've ever heard of, and a man like Gabriel would never believe it was by chance. Hell, I hardly believe it myself.

I hold his intense stare and pray my heartbeat won't betray me. "I'm not a spy. And I don't care for your tone."

He leans even closer. "How did you end up here?" The vibrations of his low baritone resonate deep in my soul.

"If you must know, I was taken prisoner by those icy bastards and beheaded them." Adrenaline tumbles in my veins, but I keep my voice steady. I'm no stranger to violence and intimidation, but I'm a fish in fucking space opposite the alpha who's clearly a force of law in this town.

The heat of his breath rushes down my neck. "What did they want from you?"

"Some demons want to own a woman like me. Those vamps were not the first to try nor will they be the last."

Gabriel wraps a hand around my right thigh, his fingertips slipping below the hem of denim. "Some women prefer to be owned."

A brutal shiver lances up my back. "Not me." *Not ever again.*

He eases his grip. "And why do you want to stay?"

"Are you kidding? Where better to hide from vampires than a werewolf stronghold?" I answer truthfully.

Despite all the wrong pop-culture info out there, the feud between vamps and werewolves is real.

Gabriel cracks a smile. The tension in his body dissipates, and he steps back, the imprint of his hand on my thigh prickling. Each nail left a separate crescent groove in the skin.

I exhale loudly. The scary-as-shit section of this program is over. "You really don't like me."

"Your aloofness is annoying, and I'm afraid you'll turn my wolves' brains into mush."

"But you'll let me stay?"

Gabriel appraises me for a moment. "Yes. But while you're here, you work for me, and you have to promise not to play them against each other."

Should I stay? Gabriel might change his mind, but after what just happened, I'm pretty sure there's nowhere on Earth that's farther from Ludovic's grasp.

I'll take hot wolves over the chilling alternative, even if my secrets might get me killed. "I'm all for everybody getting along." My eyes trail down the alpha's rugged body. He's not quite as tall as Sam, but larger, fuller.

Pushing my powers forward, I envelop Gabe in what I like to call my hypnotic stick-of-candy haze.

Our lips are a hair apart when he squeezes the back of my neck and holds me in place. "I don't have to kiss you to know what kind of man I am." His smoldering stare tightens my skin into goosebumps, but he draws back and walks away unperturbed. Like I haven't just given him everything I've got, and he hasn't just proved that he's the most powerful creature I've ever encountered.

Holy hell.

THE SCIENTIST

SAM

*V*icky hops down from Gabriel's pick-up truck, and the knot in my windpipe loosens. If he'd killed her, Dom would have blown a gasket. Hell, I would have been upset, but I trust my alpha on matters of pack security.

Our gazes meet over the green railings running around the house, and she joins me on the back porch. Dusk is settling in, whiffs from the spaghetti sauce I left on the stove filling the air with tomatoes and spices.

Dom's shirt is gone, replaced by a skirt and a red and black top that accents all her curves. The unfastened buttons of her blouse allow a wide view of her cleavage, and I can't help but notice how the fabric hugs her breasts.

Her in-your-face sexuality should bother me. Hell, it does bother me. But it should bother me *more*.

Guilt pinches my heart.

After years and years of grief, followed by a numb period, this is the first woman who makes me want to break the promise I made to myself when Sybil died. The first time my wolf howls for a mate. But it's not real. Vicky has that effect on every guy she crosses paths with.

She sits beside me on the step. "Stay with me for a sec?" There's no lust seeping through her fingers when she places her hand over my arm.

The shaky tone gives me pause.

She rubs her arms with her hands, goosebumps making every hair on her body stand up even though the evening is nice and warm. "You knew. Earlier, when Gabriel asked me to come with him. You knew I might not come back."

"Yes."

Her throat bobs.

The guilt from earlier turns into a raging inferno. "If you'd been a spy..."

She shushes me with one long, haunted look. "We just met, but I assumed you cared about your patients enough not to send them out to be assassinated without so much as a warning." Her voice trembles. "My bad. I know better than to trust strange men. Even the nice ones." She dusts off her butt and stands.

I run after her and block her escape with a gentle pull. "I'm sorry."

Her hand comes between us. She flattens it to my chest over my quickened, delirious heart. She clearly intended on shoving me away, but she's frozen. I reach up but only manage to cover her small hand with mine and squeeze hard. Our chests rise and fall for a couple of ragged breaths while we both stare, entranced, at our joined hands.

I remind myself this isn't some special connection. It's simple biology.

But then, why is she so breathless?

Why do I feel like I betrayed her?

Like she said: we just met.

And she's with Dom.

Gabriel clears his throat, shattering the moment. "Inside. Now. We need to talk."

A hint of red sears Vicky's cheeks. "Do you order everyone around like that?"

"Yes, and it includes you. Come," Gabriel says.

She digs her heels in the lawn. "Why not talk here?"

"The woods have ears. I won't ask a third time."

She growls, and the sound is both menacing and totally bewitching. "What's the magic word?"

"Fuck you, Blondie."

Right when I think she's about to run for her life, her posture relaxes, and she laughs. "Good enough."

We all enter the house, and Gabriel closes the door behind us.

Dom is back from his fool's errand. He has no idea why he was sent away, and I don't plan on telling him. With some luck, she'll have the good sense not to say anything.

Gabriel leans against a large wood beam. "I asked around. Your kidnappers were from the Pereira clan."

"Then I better cancel my trip to Brazil," she says in jest.

Gabriel chucks out a laugh. "Indeed."

I tap my index finger to my mouth. "How long do you figure they might look for you? How long will you stay?"

"How long will you have me?"

Dom strokes her upper arm. "They want you that bad, eh?"

"I attracted the wrong kind of attention, and now I killed three of them. That probably raised my profile." Her humor rings false, and a few beads of sweat form on her forehead.

I bite the insides of my cheeks. "But they were heading North. Not South."

She shrugs.

The Pereiras are known for being artists not slavers. And Northern California is too cold for them, so why the hell were they up *here*? We've never had any issues with them, and I'm not even sure they know we exist. But Gabriel is already suspicious of her as it is, and I don't want to make things harder for her, so I keep my questions and doubts to myself.

"They have an APB out on you and the car. Of course, they won't find anything," Gabriel explains. "But they are looking."

"Fine, fine. You don't have to beg. I'm moving in." Her gaze shifts from the ground to the counter and back again, never meeting ours.

"And if they were to visit..." Dom taps the beam with his knuckles. "I haven't ripped a vampire's head off in months."

He relishes the violence. Always.

Vicky plants an unbridled kiss on his mouth, and I feel it again. This unreasonable pang of jealousy. This urge to step forward to kiss her slender, perfectly smooth neck and tell Dom to fuck off.

My alpha glares from the other side of the happy couple, and I look down, my cheeks more flushed than a teenager caught masturbating. He motions for me to follow him outside.

The air is still charged with humidity and guilt, the deck's planks whining under our combined weight.

"Don't tell me you're getting soft on her, too," Gabe grumbles.

I stare at the remnants of the sunset falling over the hill, the woods—our woods—towering in the distance. I wonder if he realizes how close we are to ruin. "How long have we been drifting apart, Gabe?"

He arches a brow. "What are you babbling about?"

"Dom wanders off alone deeper and deeper into the woods. I don't go out of the house anymore. You've retreated into your dark cloud routine ever since Evelyn left."

"We're still a pack. We'll always be a pack."

"We need a common goal."

Gabriel shakes his head. "That *girl* is not here to heal us, Sam."

"Why not?"

He scratches his jaw. "Did you bump your head or something? We can barely share a ketchup bottle without it turning into a brawl."

A fierce heat spreads in my chest. "I wasn't saying we'd *share* her." Gabriel's comment ripples across my chest, my heart, my stomach. "I'd never assume..."

"Oh, don't give me that look. It's clearly what she wants. She's a sex demon ready to sink her teeth into three hot werewolves. She'll chew you up and spit you out if you're not careful. Both of you."

"Not you? Because I haven't seen anyone rile you up this way since—" I rush through the last part, doing a quick bit of math in my head. Has it really been seven years? God...

Gabriel huffs, "She's an impatient child who thinks she's God's gift to men. I'm not interested in the least."

"You're selling her short. There's more to her than that. Her flippant behavior is clearly a defense mechanism."

His gaze darts to the sky. "That'll teach me to turn a man who has a PhD in psychology."

"I got it after you bit me."

He motions loosely to my head. "Yeah, but you were the type."

"You saved me. You saved Dom. Now, we save her."

He raises his hand dismissively. "She doesn't need saving. We're just a convenient hideout."

I shrug, knowing we'll have to agree to disagree.

"Sammy?"

I meet his gaze. "Mm?"

"Whatever you do, I don't care, but don't fall for her." He pats my shoulder in both an affectionate and condescending manner before marching off to the forest.

MISERY BUSINESS

VICKY

"*O*w." A small voice says.

"Don't move, Payton. It'll be over in a minute," Sam answers.

I borrowed Sam's car and found a small women's clothing store. (Yay me, I found a bra!) I dump my new clothes on the couch and peek into the exam room.

A girl is sitting on a stool, her white knuckles braced between her thighs while Sam stitches her neck. She's looks about fifteen years old, her dirty blond hair tied above her head in a messy bun. Her forehead is creased, and she's biting her lip.

Sam's hands move with ease. He's not wearing gloves, but other than that he looks very professional. "I remember my first few changes. They're hard to control."

The teenager grumbles. "Exactly. I don't know why everyone is giving me such a hard time."

"Kudos for your fighting skills. Sean was in bad shape," Sam chuckles.

Payton cranes her neck around to look at him. "Really?"

He cuts the thread. "Yes, but maybe you don't tear half his shoulder off next time? It's a lot of stitches."

"Okay." She swerves from left to right. "Is Dominic around?"

Sam dumps his soiled instruments into a metal container. "He's sleeping."

"Oh."

The room is dark, x-rays of a spine hanging on the illuminator, and I knock on the open door.

Payton glares at my yellow sundress. "My mother said you were *pretty*."

"And?" I chose this outfit to lure Sam out of the house. It's cute instead of sexy. Non-threatening. I can't dress like a man eater every day of the week.

The girl rakes her black nails against her ripped jeans. "You're okay. If you like the Barbie-doll type."

The envy in her tone is hard to miss.

"You're into Dominic," I guess.

"What? No." She sneaks a glance at Sam, her face redder than a freshly painted fire hydrant.

"I understand. He's really hot," I admit.

Sam raises a brow. "Is he, now?"

I lean towards his patient in a conspiratorial manner. "Sam is jealous."

Even though I'm muted, Payton's pupils widen. She scratches her elbow and jumps to her feet. "Eww. Sam is old."

"I'll take that as a thank you," he says sarcastically.

Her nose wrinkles in obvious shame. "Thank you, Doc."

His eyes soften. "You're welcome. Now, take it easy for a few days."

"Will do." She skips off.

Once the front door closes behind her, I turn to the handsome doctor. "Why are the others living in town and leading normal lives while you and Dom stay here? It's not like you can't afford a house."

"I prefer to live here." The stiffness in his shoulders speaks volumes.

"Why?" I examine the suture kit. Needles and thread are wrapped individually in little packets.

"It's close to work." His tone is quiet and tight like I'm picking at a painful scab.

I back off. "What about Dom?"

Sam sits at his desk and starts typing. "Dom is new."

"He told me he'd been bitten a decade ago."

"Exactly, he's still a pup. The first few years..." Sam pauses, his lips tucked between his teeth. "The change consumes you."

I trace the collar of his shirt. "And you?"

He shrugs me off. "I'm not new."

"You're impossible." I hop on his desk. "What are we doing today?" I ask, dangling my bare legs from the edge.

He pries a lab report from under my ass. "*I* am working."

"Can I stay and help?"

After stealing a glance at my knees, he snorts and gives me an *I'm not stupid* look.

"Fine. I'll go for a walk then. It's nice outside." I yank the curtains away from the big floor-to-ceiling windows, and the bright sunlight washes over the dark room.

Sam shields his face with his hand. "Keep to the east. The west side is the pups' training ground, and the trails to the north are worse than a labyrinth."

With a cute tilt of the head, I tug on his sleeve. "Be my guide? Come on. Sun is shining, birds are chirping, it's a zip-a-dee-do-dah day. Your paperwork can spare a minute."

His chest heaves. He looks out at the twinkling forest and raises his index finger. "One hour."

I beam and follow in his wake. He ditches the white coat and reveals a slim-fit blue dress shirt. Yummy, but a little stuffy for a summer walk in the woods.

There's an acre or two of empty fields directly behind the house, but on the east side, the forest creeps close to the wrap-around porch. The trees aren't closely knit together, though, and the path is wide and well-traveled.

Leaves crack under my soles. I wait a few minutes before chatting Sam up, letting him soak in a bit of sun and fresh air. I get the feeling he spends way too much time in that stuffy office of his. "Since you won't tell me *when* you were born, can you tell me *where*?"

"I was born in Pittsburgh."

"And where are we, exactly?" I've been playing it cool since Gabriel's interrogation, but I need to know.

"Oregon."

Oregon. It makes no sense. If the vampires were taking me to Europe, why head north-west? I wrack my brain for an explanation.

A serious pout twists Sam's features. "Where were the Pereiras taking you?"

Oh my wolf! He's a mind reader. "No idea."

"I won't tell Gabriel."

"Thank you, but I really don't know." I smack my lips together. "I went to the store this morning to buy a few essentials, and I got the feeling that you don't get a lot of visitors."

Sam unbuttons his cuff-links and hikes his sleeves up to his elbows. "We don't. And especially not these days."

"Am I that special?"

"Very." The hushed word, along with the shy glance he throws me, quickens my heart. He's not *too* shy nor *playing* shy, which is hard to balance. "Don't blame Gabriel for being suspicious. I mean— you looked so perfect lying there..."

I scoff. "I looked perfect lying on the side of the road with half my guts hanging out? That's a first."

"Okay, maybe not *perfect*."

I elbow his side. "Hey! Don't take this away from me."

A gentle laugh ripples through the both of us, each giggle warming my chest.

Shadows create intricate patterns on the ground. We head deeper into the woods, but what we get in shade costs us in the gentle breeze we had, and the humidity thickens. It's late summer, so bugs aren't as much of a nuisance as I expected. The path cleaves in three different trails, and Sam explains where each leads. His shoulders wiggle as he speaks.

A few minutes later, he shrugs his shirt off. "It's really hot."

"Yeah. Really hot." But the heat lacing down my spine has nothing to do with the weather, and my mouth waters.

He's taller and leaner than Dominic, so somehow my brain didn't do the math right and expected his muscles to be lacking, but the doctor is shredded. He's got the touch *and* the look. I'd love for him to keep me warm at night.

Chiseled eight-pack abs with light chest hair and sculpted arms spark my hunger anew. A defined Adonis belt disappears under the waistband of his dark jeans, and I want to lick it on my way down to his cock. Like now.

He strolls down the most overshadowed trail, oblivious to my newfound obsession.

I snatch his hand to stop his stride. "Wait."

"Are you tired? We can take a shortcut back to—"

Desire rumbling in my belly, I trace a path from his navel to the V-shaped furrow and hook my fingers under the denim. A thin film of sweat shines off his torso, and I push my powers forward, giving him a nice sample of what is sure to be an unforgettable nature fuck.

A sigh parts his lips. "I was afraid you'd do this."

The need in my stomach collapses into stone.

He hooks the shirt around his elbow, and his gorgeous blue eyes pulse with emotion. "It's at least a hundred degrees. I was actually overheating in that thing."

"I believe you." My throat is tight. I can't handle another failure.

Lust darkens his eyes, his fist curling at his side. "It wasn't a ploy to seduce you."

"I know. I'm seduced anyway."

"You barely know me."

A heavy lump wedges itself in my throat. "I'm not liking the judgment in your voice, mister. Slut-shaming isn't okay."

He walks away, breathing heavily.

I run after him. "You want me. I want you. We're both single. Let's be adults about this."

He spins around to face me. "Let's! You've spent too much time with people who only expect sex from you, that it's like you've forgotten how to feel anything else. I'm more than a piece of meat you can just *chew* up."

The words resonate somewhere deep in my soul. Somewhere private. They ripple across a scar that will never heal, and I bite the insides of my cheeks. "Oh yeah? Well, you're a repressed prude who missed out of the best head of his life!"

"You made my point." He storms off the beaten path and disappears into the wild.

I press my tongue against the roof of my mouth and swallow the damn tears that sting my eyes. He can judge me all he wants. I don't need him or his old-fashioned bullshit. I don't need to be reminded how ugly this unending struggle is.

Men. Women. Humans. Demons. They all want me, but they make me feel cheap. Dirty. Like my need for sex is disgraceful. Men who sleep around are called players; I'm called worse.

Ever since I discovered I was a vandella, I've had to put up with this shit.

I've heard it all.

"I want you, but—" "I love you, but—" There's always a fucking *but*. "It's because of what you are." "It's not real."

It's never real to them. To any of them. They all rush off in search of *real* love.

They never stop to realize... it's real to me.

It's the only reality I'll ever know.

FULL MOON

VICKY

To my extreme annoyance, I find myself unable to sleep that night, even after a nice Dominic sundae. I toss and turn in his bed, rehashing what Sam said. I've got everything that I need right here. Why do I care if that damn doctor isn't into casual sex? It's not like I need a man to validate my sexuality.

Dom's palms travel up my bare back. "What's bothering you?"

I press my check into the pillow and close my eyes, his hands tending to a knot in my shoulder. "Nothing."

"Tell me."

"Sam. He said some things." My voice is muffled by the sheets.

The nice massage stops. "You made a move on him."

"You don't mind, do you?" I crane my neck around to watch his expression.

His lips curl up. "No. Hell, Sam needs to have a little fun. He's almost as stiff as the boss. But a word of advice. If you want to get into Sam's pants, don't push him."

The rigid ache in my chest loosens up. Dominic is a breath of fresh air. No lies. No pretenses. He doesn't need for this thing between us to be labeled or to fit into some mold. He's happy discovering it day by day. "Why is Sam so..."

Dom grins. "Stuck-up?"

I snort. "I was going to say *inhibited*."

"Sure you were. Sam is the most affluent werewolf that doesn't have a mate. Besides Gabe, of course. Shifter politics are dirty and medieval. Think Game of Thrones meets Desperate Housewives. As the most powerful bachelor, Sam's a catch. Girls have been throwing themselves at him for years. He's become touchy about it."

Wow. Maybe our fight wasn't all about me. "And he always says no?"

"He thinks—and he's mostly right—that they are only after his position. And a part of him is still—" Dom stops abruptly.

I don't know if the fact that Sam has been celibate for years is discouraging or fuck-hot. From the knot in my stomach and the fuzzy flutters in my heart, I'd say the latter.

Dom rolls on his stomach. "Since you can't sleep, go talk to him. He's probably outside reading. He always does that when he's upset."

Unable to stop myself, I shuffle out of bed, wrap one of Dominic's hoodies around my frame, and look for Sam outside, resolute on not coming on to him.

The night is warm and still. There's not even a whiff of wind disturbing the leaves of the lonely oak underneath which Sam is sitting. The large canopy casts shadows on the wet grass.

"Don't you sleep?" I ask.

The doctor rests his book on the tartan blanket, his fingers marking the page. "I've never been a big sleeper."

"Dom barely made it out of bed before supper yesterday. I thought it was a wolf thing."

"Dom is Dom," he says with a gentle laugh.

I get a glimpse of the affection he feels for his fellow wolf. "You like him a lot."

"He's family to me."

Our eyes meet, a heavy silence filling the gaps.

"I never wanted to imply I thought you were a..." Sam's jaw clenches, "You're not a slut. But I'm not a prude. We're just... different. There's no wrong or right."

A dry snicker grates my throat. "Society would disagree."

"Society sucks. I'm just saying that I'm not—I can't separate sex and feelings. It's not me." His gaze falls to the empty space next to him.

I fold my legs beneath me, and, after making sure I'm completely muted, I nudge his side with my elbow. "I'm sorry I acted like you were a piece of meat."

He nudges me right back. "I'm sorry I gave you hell for it. It must be hard. To have to *feed* every day."

"Sometimes it is," I admit, shedding a piece of my armor. "Though I'd love to *chew* you up someday."

"Stick around then. I'm like cheese."

"You mean you'll eventually start to stink?" I tease, understanding perfectly well what he meant.

He laughs. "Maybe that was an unwise metaphor. I should have gone with wine."

The millions of stars twinkling above us fill me with joy. I'm not used to the calm immensity of a clear night sky or the vast quietness of the woods. I'm a city girl, a social butterfly. Heels and cocktails. Pavement and crime.

"You look star-stuck," Sam says, "Literally."

"I don't see a lot of stars in the city."

"Where are you from?"

"LA. The entire population of Wolf Creek would probably fit in my old high-rise." The hustle and glittering lights of Los Angeles provided the perfect cover. In a city so glamorous and over-the-top, people didn't notice me as much. They saw make-up instead of golden eyelashes. Aspiring model instead of demonic curves. No one batted an eye at my purple irises. Blending in became a question of survival, but it went against my nature, so I added nomad to my list of qualities. Never staying in one place long. Almost never building lasting relationships.

Here, everyone knows everyone, and a part of me is curious to know what it feels like.

The heat emanating from Sam brings goosebumps to my neck.

The weird pull is back, so tangible that I can almost feel a string knot around my heart, tying us together. It's a strange sensation, and while I'm wary of men having such an effect on me, I know it's something I can't control. And I want to hang on to this feeling because it's rare and fleeting.

"What were you reading?" I ask quickly so I don't blurt out a bad joke.

"A thriller."

I peek to see if he's telling the truth. "Ah! I thought you were going to say poetry."

"Poetry's dull."

I snort and press my nose to his shoulder. The light touch is enough to squeeze my stomach. His sweet-but-spicy scent is to die for, but I'll be good. I'll give him enough time to get soft and tasty if that's what he wants.

I don't buy for a second that women only hit on him for his position in the pack. With his natural charisma, he could bring any girl to her knees.

When I peel myself from the blanket, he squeezes my hand. "Goodnight, Vicky."

"Goodnight, Sam."

THE NIGHT AFTER THAT, I look for Sam on the grass again, but he's not there. Still, I lay a blanket down and sprawl out to look at the sky.

I hike up to my elbows when a wolf struts in my direction. It's big, 200 pounds of raw muscle prowling towards me, but I'm not worried.

His fur is pale but thick, his eyes one hundred percent Sam. I hold out my hand when he wanders close, and he sniffs it.

He curls up at the edge of the blanket.

I inch my hand closer to him. "Can I?"

He rests his head on his paws.

A grin curls my lips as I pet him. "You're so soft."

A small cooing sound is followed by a big yawn.

"You can understand me, right?"

He nods, and it cracks me up to see such an imposing animal nod his head so casually.

I straighten up when I feel the familiar pressure of a stranger's gaze prickling my skin. "Someone's watching us."

Sam springs to his feet, but his predatory stance quickly melts into something I'd call quiet annoyance. His tail twitches rapidly, and his ears are still pointing down, but he covers his teeth.

A man about Dom's height prances over to us, stark naked. He's buff, but somehow his proportions aren't as flattering. Oily hair is brushed back on his head, and his teeth are simply too big. The sum of it all makes him look a little weird, but from his roaring confidence and half-smirk, I figure he hasn't got the memo.

My jaw is skewed. I'm used to nudity, but there's something plain wrong about a stranger prancing over to you with his junk bouncing about, and I keep my eyes firmly planted on his forehead.

His gaze falls to Sam. "Hey, Doc." He licks his lips and extends his hand. "Dave DeLuca."

"Vicky." I mute my powers as I shake it. I hold them back hard and wish I could give off an *anti-sex* vibe. I'm grateful for the large hoodie hanging from my shoulders.

A heavy leer skims my bare thighs. "Vicky..."

"That's all of it," I clip.

The derisive chuckle that follows makes my blood boil.

"No last name? You're like Cher."

"Or Madonna."

Dominic swings the porch door open wide and half-runs towards us. The wet grass brushes against the edge of his pajama pants, his feet bare, and he puts himself between me and the newcomer. "DeLuca. What are you doing here at this hour?"

DeLuca steps back an inch. "Romano. Heard there was a novelty in town. Came to see it for myself."

It. Not she. The jab is as impolite and deliberate as one can be.

The man motions in the general direction of me and Sam. "I heard you were the lucky one, but I see I've been misinformed."

Dom growls.

DeLuca holds both his palms up. "Or not."

"Gabriel wants to see you inside." Both rows of teeth accompany the message, though the expression on Dom's face can't qualify as a smile.

We all watch him retreat inside the house, and I rub my arms to erase the chilly effect of the creepy werewolf's presence.

Dom taps his palm on his forehead. "He's sooooo annoying. I can't pee in the woods without him sniffing it the next day." He wraps his arms around me, his hot skin scattering small shivers all over my body. "DeLuca is the noisiest neighbor in history."

I raise a brow. "He doesn't come off as a 'nosy neighbor' to me. I got a definitive 'dangerous psycho' whiff."

Dom places a butterfly kiss on my neck. "DeLuca is the worst, but he knows his place."

I'm not convinced. Not in the least.

I THINK I'M PARANOID

VICKY

"You call that a sandwich?" Dominic asks as he pries open my breakfast, lifting the top slice of bread into the air.

I frown. "What's wrong with it? It's lettuce, tomato and ham between two pieces of bread."

"One *tiny* slice of ham. You live with wolves. You have an entire array of delicious proteins at your disposal." He yanks open the fridge door and slides the meat tray toward him. "Ham. Roast beef, pastrami, turkey, smoked-meat, salami, *and* pepperoni."

Sam chuckles from his seat. "Uh-oh. You woke the beast."

I watch, curious, as Dom starts buttering a piece of bread. "I'll show you what a real sandwich should taste like."

Leaning over the island on my elbows, I smile. "Should you warn me about another facet of your personality? Or is this obsession with luncheon meat your only quirk?"

Dom wets his lips. "I'm full of surprises, baby."

I giggle and throw a piece of rye bread at his face.

He gobs it in mid-air and dashes closer for a kiss, switching my plate for another, my new sandwich bursting at the seams.

Gabriel roars into the kitchen, interrupting our fun bickering. "Morning, underlings. I have to go out of town today, so let's expedite this meeting. First order of business. Our free-loading guest."

I almost choke on a mouthful of pastrami.

The alpha's eyes are bright, and a sarcastic smile tugs at the corners of his full lips.

I fluff my hair and angle my body to him, making sure the satin robe I'm wearing reveals too much.

The smirk disappears. "I made a list of things for you to do while I'm gone. I should be back for dinner tomorrow, so that'll give you plenty of time." He hands me a piece of paper.

I skim the list. He mentioned something about working for him, but— "Dishes, groceries, folding laundry? Can you be more misogynistic?" My eyes budge. "I'm not your maid!"

"No. Jillian is our maid, and she's sick. You can step in just this once. And don't run your mouth off for nothing." He points to the last line. "Cutting wood for the fire and taking out the trash. There. Manly."

"What fire? It's stuffy outside."

"I like to be prepared," Gabriel answers.

The three of them are doing a poor job at stifling their laughter.

"Fuck you all!"

"It's not on the list. You'll be way too busy to fuck anyone." The alpha glares down at me with unparalleled intensity. "This isn't a five star resort. We all work for a living, and if you want to stay in my town, then, so will you."

My fist curls, and I'm about to punch his big mouth when Dom tugs on my arm.

"Come on. It's no big deal. Just a few chores," he says, trying to keep the peace.

I bite the insides of my cheeks. "I don't do chores."

Sam raises a brow. "Not ever?"

"Nope."

Dom pinches the note. "Alright, I can do some after I help John with his cattle. But Gabe is right. You're spoiled."

"Spoiled!" I tear the list from his hands. "I can do all of this with my eyes closed." I stomp to the bedroom to change.

Gabriel is gone when I come back, and I start with the wood cutting, purging the anger out of me one swing at a time. A pissed vandella with an axe can do some damage, but I'm not quite mad enough to chop down the house into little pieces and set it on fire. Yet.

After a lot of scrubbing and a quick shower, I take care of the trash. The grocery store is my last stop.

The building takes up the whole corner lot. There's no recognizable brand on it, only a big sign spelling *Fred's Corner* in big red letters.

Once inside, I realize it's also the pharmacy and the post office, so I'll save eons of time. The fruit and vegetable section is rudimentary, but the products are fresh.

Before I know it, I'm cornered by three female werewolves. They all look to be in their mid-thirties to early forties, wearing sports clothes like they just came from the gym.

"Ladies." I nod, sizing up the situation.

"What are you still doing here?" A tall one seethes.

Three of them. One of me. This could get dicey. "Grocery shopping."

They walk around me in circles. "You think you're so smart."

"Sometimes." I play the cool cucumber, but I'm more of a distraught apple.

Since they aren't human, my lure isn't as effective, and the hateful vibe rolling off them convinces me to crank my powers way down. They're not secretly yearning for an out-of-the-box sexual experience, and I'm definitely not looking to get mauled by an angry pack of wolves.

I brace my hands on my hips. "Okay. What's the deal, here? Who shouldn't I fuck? Because I'm already fucking Dominic, so it can't be him. Afraid your alpha will take a liking to me?"

The oldest one snickers, "Gabriel would never touch you."

"So, this is about Sam," I surmise.

The one with blond hair growls, "Sam's been through a lot. Stay away from him."

A fourth one with electric blue highlights and an eyebrow piercing skitters around the edge of the hate circle like she's looking for a reason to interrupt.

Insults blur into one another.

"City whore."

"Demon filth."

"Skank."

A forceful push takes me by surprise, and I drop my oranges. My knees bend slightly as I brace myself for another, ready to strike back. I'll break an arm; I don't care. A vicious laughter echoes along the industrial cooling bins before the women filter out.

I pick up the fruits and sigh. Bullied at the grocery store... how the mighty have fallen.

The punk-rock chick kneels to help me. She's younger. A few pimples still plague her skin, but she's a beauty. Dark, straight hair cascades down her back, and her green eyes are striking. "Don't mind them," she says, her glossy red lips pursed into a pout.

I spot her name tag. M. Dawson.

"I'm Lena." She wipes her hands on her jeans. "I'm 19, by the way."

Leading with her age. Subtle.

"Vicky." I point to the M above her breast. "What's the M for?"

She rolls her eyes. "My dad had the inspired idea of calling me *Magdalena*." She chucks out the name like it's He-Who-Shall-Not-Be-Named.

"This town gets crazier by the minute," I joke.

"Oh, we're not crazy. We do hate female strangers, especially sexy demons who threaten the shallow pool of available bachelors." Her spirited eyes brim with fire. "I heard about what you are."

"And?"

"I see why everyone's all freaked out..." Blood floods her cheeks, but she meets my gaze head-on. "They figure you're a temptress who came straight from an evil corner of hell to steal their first-borns and make it rain frogs or something."

I throw my head back and laugh but hold on tight to my lure. This girl's got spunk, and if I have a chance of making a female friend in this damn unfriendly town, I don't want to ruin it. "God, I need a drink. Is there any fun place to hang out around here?"

"What do you think? This town is populated with people who were born before television was invented."

"So no club in town, eh?"

A big sigh passes her lips. "Not even a fun place to dance. Not for another century. I can't wait to turn 20 and get out of here."

"How do you survive in the meantime?" I'm no fool. Girls, even wolves, just want to have fun.

"We thrown mean parties at the falls once a month. And Springfield's got a few nice hangouts. It's less than an hour's drive."

"We should go. Tonight." I raise a brow, daring her to accept.

She peeks over her shoulders, scanning the room quickly, and leans in. "Haven't you heard? We're all on curfew. None of us can leave town without Gabriel's permission."

A tall man opens the door behind the meat counter and clears his throat.

"See you around, Vicky." With the distinct expression of a kid caught doing something wrong, Lena skips to the employees section.

My knuckles turn white against the plump orange I'm still holding. What the hell is going on in this town? I've been operating under the assumption that Gabriel wants to get rid of me, but is leaving even an option? Maybe my choices are playing maid or pushing up daisies.

After a quick stop at the cash register where a sullen woman takes notes of what I took instead of actually asking for money, I throw the groceries in the back seat and explore the town. There's a school, a library, a gas station, a big warehouse, a couple of other stores and a few restaurants. Many roads snake off into the woods. When I cross a sign for Springfield, I press down the accelerator.

A police barrage is waiting for me half a mile down the road, a big truck blocking the path leading to the regional road. My foot cramps as I consider crushing the pedal down to risk an escape. The sight of a spiked strip of tire shredders quickens my pulse.

I stop and roll my window down.

"Hello, there." The policeman drawls. He's tall and angular with a balding hairline.

"Can you help me, officer? I think I lost my way." I bat my eyelashes at him. Can't hurt.

He points to the way I came. "Make a u-turn and take a right at the stop. You should find your way back after that."

"Thanks." I put the car in gear.

The man grips the window, each of his nails scratching against the glass. "A word of advice, Miss No-Last-Name?"

"Mm?"

A smirk slowly spreads on his lips, and the vivid image of a shark superimposes over my vision. "Don't get lost again."

My reciprocating smile is 1000% fake.

I hurry back to the cabin, my mind reeling. Where's my phone? Clearly, they found it. How come they didn't give it back?

Now that I think about it, I haven't see anyone use a smart phone since I've been here.

I explore the lavish home with new eyes, searching for clues. The front half is divided between Sam's exam room and Gabriel's office and followed by the open kitchen and living room. There's a bathroom and two bedrooms in the back, so Gabriel must sleep in the basement. A solid wood door beckons from the foot of the staircase.

Sam sneaks up on me. "Don't go down there." His warning is laced with fear. "Gabriel catches you down there, he'll kill you."

I grip the banister. "Gabriel is out of town."

"Doesn't matter. He'll smell your trail."

Chewing on my bottom lip, I look deep inside Sam's blue eyes, searching for the truth. "What's down there? His room? Or something else?"

He tilts his head to the side. "Why do you want to know?"

"Where is my phone?"

"Gabriel has it."

Uh-huh. I clamp my mouth shut. I can't give any more weight to the spy theory before I figure out what to do.

Dom yanks open the porch door, buck naked, providing a nice distraction. "Evening."

"Any trouble?" Sam asks.

"Nope." Dom beelines for the shower, leaving a strong whiff of grass and sweat in his wake.

Sam grabs a knife and a cutting board. "I'll make dinner."

"I'll help you." I steal glances at Sam while we cook. I underestimated him once, so I don't want to let my hormones get in the way of my good sense. I unpack the groceries and try to push my suspicions to the back of my mind.

Dom pats his hair dry with a white towel and grabs a beer in the fridge. "What are we eating, woman?" From the huge grin on his face, I know he's yanking my chain.

After supper, I head inside Dom's room, and he follows. I block his path with my body, bracing my arm against the door frame. "Since I'm not on vacation, as you so selflessly reminded me this morning, I want a room. To myself."

He frowns. "There's no free room."

"Then you can sleep on the couch tonight." I shut the door in his face and snicker under my breath. That'll teach him to take Mr. Serious Alpha's side over mine. Whatever is going on here, Dom and Sam might not be in on it. Dom is too free with his words, too enthusiastic. And Sam is too... Sam. But I can't be sure, so I need unsupervised access to a computer. I have to figure out what's going on.

But the firewall prevents me from sending any information out to the web. No emails. No Facebook. No nothing.

Wave after wave of dread unfurls in my stomach, a long-feared but familiar feeling clawing its way up my throat.

Whether they know it or not, I'm a prisoner.

A CROSS AND A GIRL NAMED BLESSED

DOMINIC

"*W*hat is going on here?" Vicky flicks me awake.

My arm is hanging from the side of the couch, and I straighten up to rub my face. "What?"

She hugs her frame, her fists balled. "Don't play dumb. I'm not up for a drawn-out battle of wills against you guys. If I'm a prisoner, I might as well know the rules."

The stink of fear rolls off her skin and awakens the predator inside me. "Hold on." I wave her closer and put my feet to the floor. I don't know what happened to her, but I need to make it all better and fast before my wolf starts rattling too hard against his cage.

She stares me up and down, her face unreadable, before taking a tentative step closer. She's still wearing her clothes from earlier.

I grab both her hands in mine. Her small fingers are cold. "What happened to you?"

"Why did Gabriel leave, and why is the town on lock-down?"

Ushering her into my lap, I wrap my arms around her, trying to appease the both of us. Her rushed heartbeats are like free-flowing wine, and I feel dizzy. "It's not about you. There's been some serious threats from the neighboring pack."

She presses her palms to my chest like she's about to push me away. "What kind of threats?"

I suck in a deep breath. "Calm down, baby. Can't expect a wolf to chat you up while you give off so much fear. Give it a minute." I caress the small of her back until she relaxes against me. The sweaty, heady scent recedes. "The opposing pack is causing trouble. The bastards swelled their ranks over the last few years, and lately they've been sniffing around for a chance to seize power. Gabriel is trying to avoid a war, but I'm not sure he can." My throat itches. One part of me is dying for a bloodbath. How great would it feel to kill the man who threatens our peace? I'd gladly sink my teeth into Xavier's neck and rip him to shreds. Without their alpha, the other wolves would have to fall in line.

Vicky's hands travel up my shoulders, and she plays with the hair at the back of my neck. "If it's not about me, why can't I leave town?"

The sexy, scornful pout glazing her lips is irresistible, and I dive in for a quick kiss. "You make them nervous. They think you might be spying for the other team."

She draws back. "So, it's a sport now?"

"You know what I mean." I lie back on the couch, pulling her with me.

After a few wiggles, she says, "I hate to feel trapped."

"You're not. I promise. It's a temporary measure, and since you're not a spy, you have nothing to worry about."

Her cheek rubs against my bare chest.

We doze off, and when I open my eyes again, the sun is streaming through the windows.

I pepper kisses on my girl's neck to coax her awake. "Are you feeling better?"

"Not really. I've been thinking about what you said. The creep from last night, he's involved."

"DeLuca?"

She sits up. "I have a sixth sense about this stuff."

I consider her words carefully. "Alright. DeLuca is Gabe's treasurer or whatever. He'll probably be all alone at the office today. We could swing by and see what he's up to. If he's a traitor, he'll probably take advantage of Gabe's absence to do something bad."

"Okay." She squeezes my hand. "Thank you for trusting me."

"Sure." She goes to change while I heat up some coffee.

I have a few errands to run first, so I pick up the barbed wire I ordered and drop it off at Garrett's before stopping for gas. I buy a huge meat sub and a cookie at the station.

When I come back, Vicky is leaning against the car, watching the other customers stream by. Her lips quirk as I hand her half of my sinful breakfast.

She nudges me with her hip. "You've been busy, mister."

I raise a brow.

"Every girl under thirty we cross paths with gives me the 'I've been there before, he'll tire of you too,' ex-girlfriend glare."

Blood rushes to my ears, and I choke on a forced chuckle. "Is there really such a thing?"

She nods confidently. "Yes. It's almost as specific as the 'get out of the way, bitch' future-girlfriend scowl."

"I bet you don't have a lot of female friends."

She huffs, but I know I'm right.

I scratch the back of my neck. "When I moved here, after being bitten, I was a novelty."

"The hot new wolf in town."

Swallowing a mouthful, I nod. "Exactly."

"But none of them managed to keep your attention."

I appraise her reaction. Is she upset? Jealous? There's nothing but humor twinkling in her eyes.

"Now, I'm stuck with my choices. I have a bit of a reputation..." I whisper the last part in her ear.

She giggles. She doesn't mind. It tells me that I don't have to hide or sugar-coat anything, and I like that.

CITY HALL IS quiet when we arrive. It's still early, and I've got the key to the back entrance. We tiptoe down the glossy linoleum hallway.

"Here. Quick." I push her into Gabe's office and soundlessly close the door behind us. "Don't touch anything. Gabe doesn't allow anyone in here."

Vicky eyes the desk, chair and filling cabinets with interest. "But you have a key."

"I know where he keeps the spare. DeLuca should be here any minute. His office is on the other side of this door," I motion to the solid pine door separating us from the adjoining room. Most of our constructions have thick walls and doors to diminish noise pollution. It's hard to sleep when you hear your roommates snoring as though they're in your bed with you.

My eyes dart around the room. Gabriel has frugal tastes in decor, and the only useless item is a huge abstract painting hanging behind his desk.

DeLuca comes in a minute later. We hear him chat with the secretary, Theresa, before he enters his office. As if on cue, a phone rings loudly on the other side of the door.

Vicky and I hold our breaths.

"It's nothing. No need to delay our plans because some sexy chick stumbled into Romano's bed." I frown at the words. Can she be right? I mean, I hate the guy, so I can easily believe he'd betray us, but Gabriel trusts him with his life. They go way back, and loyalty is a big thing among wolves.

"He's bluffing. He doesn't know anything. He'll fall for it hook, line and sinker." A loud bang resonates like DeLuca punched his desk. "We don't have to. Yes, boss."

The whines of hinges is heard before Theresa says, "Jeff is waiting for you downstairs."

We hear footsteps and the sound of the door slamming shut.

Vicky and I exchange a glance.

"Who the hell was he talking to?" She licks her delicious red lips. "You need to keep an eye on this guy."

I nod gravely. "Let's keep this to ourselves, at least until we have proof."

She fists my collar and pulls me in for a kiss. "This spying thing is hot."

When her small hand reaches for my zipper, I peel her off me. "We can't. Not here."

She clicks her tongue and paces the room. Her slim fingers drag over the mahogany desk. She shimmies out of her underwear, bends over and wiggles her perfect ass. She's wearing a sinful school-girl miniskirt that barely covers her butt, and I gawk.

My tongue drags against the roof of my mouth. "Oh, hell. You're cheating."

She throws me a cheeky smile over her shoulder. "Come on. Be a good wolf and fuck me."

I am a weak man. Weaker still when the girl of my dreams is begging me to take her from behind on my boss' desk. My cock sings in anticipation, my rational thoughts dead in the water. Her shirt hikes up her back in this position, and I can't help but caress the arch of her spine. As soon as my fingers make contact with her smooth skin, her legs part slightly, and she offers me the most tantalizing view yet.

I bite my bottom lip and groan. "You're not fighting fair."

"Who wants fair?"

"Not me." I fumble with my zipper with one hand and sink my nails into the tender flesh of her ass with the other.

It's more than sex. She's witty, adventurous and drop-dead gorgeous. I could really fall for this girl. We'd make a hell of a team. We could pull out the broom stuck in these peoples' asses and bring them into the 21st century, starting with Sam and Gabe. I love those guys, but sometimes they can be so old-fashioned.

I push inside her, her tight heat better than I remembered. She takes every inch of me and purrs.

Every time with her gets richer and deeper. I'll never tire of it. My imagination is ablaze with all the positions and surfaces we haven't tried, yet. Gabe's desk is a pretty sweet spot. Absolutely forbidden. It's a big turn-on for me, but I wonder why she picked it.

A pencil rolls off the edge and falls to the ground as I pick up the pace. Her knuckles clench around a stack of important papers, sending Gabriel's scent into my nose, and my eyes narrow.

Vicky meets my thrusts eagerly, her eyes closed, her slit so wet and greedy that I have to wonder if she's picturing him in my place. The thought fuels my need, and I slam my hips into her. A little role-play will probably get me my answer, so I grip her hair. "You like that, Blondie?"

Her breath catches, her legs spreading even wider.

I stop abruptly, my cock barely grazing her entrance, and spank her ass, imitating Gabriel's gruff tone. "You want me to fuck you hard and fast on *my* desk?"

"Yes!"

I like that she can say it. That she's not ashamed. Hell, I'd gladly watch. Sadly, Gabe swore off intelligent women, but I know his style. Holding her down so her cheek is flat against the desk, I stretch her top down her breasts and pinch her nipple.

She bucks her hips. My cock is warm and heavy in my hand as I tease her clit with the tip until she's squirming. When I feel her ripe and ready, I crash back inside her, aiming deep like I want to etch a piece of myself into her flesh.

With a high-pitched scream, she comes hard, the pulse of her climax squeezing my shaft. Holy fucking Aphrodite. One of the most powerful orgasms of my life wrecks me, and I fill her to the brim.

I never want to go back to normal women. Never. I want to

worship her body for the rest of time. With her by my side, I'd be the happiest and luckiest wolf to ever live.

Vicky's neck beckons, and I nibble her skin. Her blood smells so incredible that my teeth pierce the first layer of skin... and I violently jerk back.

Shocked, I stagger backwards, slipping out of her. "Damn. I almost bit you. It got almost impossible not to."

She pats her neck. "It's not a big deal. It would have healed."

I quickly pull my jeans up. "It's a huge deal. Wolves only bite their mates during sex. It's more than teeth." I shudder at the thought that I almost mated with an unwitting woman that has clear commitment issues.

"I'd turn into a big bad wolf?" she says with a chuckle.

"Be serious for one second. I almost bit you while I was inside you. Once you've marked someone, you're linked for life." I nuzzle her hair.

She skips out of my reach and crosses her arms over her chest. "Are you proposing?"

"Don't joke about that. Gabriel would crucify me for even thinking about mating. I'm too young. And you'd be stuck with me forever," I explain.

"Forever is way too serious for me." She sidesteps the way a Yankee fan avoids the visiting team's supporters coming out of the urinal. "It's cold. Let's go back to the cabin."

I'M LIKE A BIRD

VICKY

"**Y**ou're thinking about leaving," Sam says.

We're laying on our blanket, looking at the stars.

"Dom told me you're on the brink of war." And he freaked me out with this whole *mate for life* scare this morning. The last thing I need is to tie myself to these wolves forever. They clearly have their own shit to work through, and they don't need my past getting in the way. If the vampires who abducted me figure out where I'm hiding, a wave of trouble will flow towards this town. I'm putting them in danger, and while the odds of being discovered are slim, nowhere is one-hundred percent safe when you're on the run from your royal vampire ex-husband.

Sam twines our fingers. "There's a fight coming. It doesn't mean you have to bolt."

"Dom mentioned a neighboring pack..."

His lips curl down. "Yes. One of our own started his own pack about seven years ago. Xavier never understood why we lived here, cut away from the human world. He wanted to build satellite communities in human cities, and many agreed with him, tired of living in a bubble. Gabriel supported their project at first, but living amongst humans isn't for everyone. The experiment was a total failure, with many wolf and human casualties. Gabriel put his foot down for Xavier to return and forget his big ideas. He refused."

"And?"

"Xavier has enough power to create his own wolves, but he struggles to keep them in check. They kill too many people and attract too much attention. Instead of starting from scratch and building his own safe haven, he wants to steal ours."

A cold patch skitters across my chest. "He wants to kill Gabriel?"

"Yes and no. He can't ask for a duel to the death and be done with it. He'd lose, for starters, but being the alpha isn't decided by brute strength. Not anymore. People believe in Gabriel." Sam rubs his chin. "This town is off the human grid. We can be ourselves, here. We don't have to worry about human justice, other shifters, or demons. Wolves can leave when they're 20, but it's at their own risk. Many return after a few years when they realize all the crap that's out there. It's also the perfect place to raise pups."

"What if a wolf leaves before that?" I ask, thinking of Lena.

"If you defy the law, you're not allowed back. 20 years old is a good age. Most of the youngsters control the shift really well by then, so there's less risk of exposure."

I scoot closer. "Do you ever leave town?"

The light in his eyes dims. "Sometimes, but not lately. Gabriel needs us here."

"What happens if Xavier wins?"

Sam's fists curl. "Gabriel built this town from scratch in the early 1900s. He'll die before letting anyone take it."

"And you?" Sam doesn't strike me as a man who likes violence.

He tugs on a rebellious weed sticking out of the blanket. "Gabriel saved my life more than once. I'll fight to the end with him."

A gust a cold air tightens my skin into goosebumps, and I rub the chill off my arms. "Not as warm as yesterday, is it?"

Sam molds his hand to mine, the calluses of his palms scattering jolts of electricity down my body.

Vampires run cold. Wolves run hot. Hotter is better, period. I lean closer to him, the heat of his body delicious against the crisp midnight air, and look up. Even sitting down, his chin is a few inches higher than the top of my head. I force myself to remain still and admire the squared line of his chiseled, masculine jaw. I'd give anything to lick its shape if he let me, but by now, I know better.

One violent shiver passes through me, and Sam finally glances down. "You don't want to be caught in a cause that's not yours. I understand."

"I'm afraid I might make things worse. You should know that—" My arms fall at my sides. "Can I help?"

He raises a hand to my neck and stokes my cheek with his thumb. My mouth dries up.

I shake as I resist the urge to make the first move.

His bottomless blue eyes stare straight into my soul, and I breathe heavily through the two-second delay as he finally, *finally*, leans in to kiss me.

Hot body. Hotter lips. Warm cocoa and mint fill my tongue. God. One taste isn't enough. I could eat nothing else for the rest of time.

I grip a handful of curls like they're the only thing connecting me to this earth and flatten my other palm to his chest. The rushed heartbeats beneath my fingers send my mind spinning.

Sam grazes my jawline on both sides and angles me to him for a deeper taste. A rugged, needy sound rumbles at the back of his throat before his tongue joins the fray. It's assertive but gentle. Experienced but out of practice.

Our mouths dance in search for the perfect rhythm. The perfect pressure. There's nothing hurried or messy about it.

It's a kiss that leaves you gasping for the next. A kiss that strips me from my usual moves, and I lose myself in the luscious depravity of it, enjoying the moment instead of jumping ahead to where kisses like that usually lead.

A prickle on my skin tells me we're being watched again. I linger in the kiss for a few more precious seconds before gently pulling back, making it seem as though I only want to gaze in Sam's eyes. "DeJerk is here."

A wild growl seeps through his teeth, and he jerks to his feet.

DeLuca strolls up to us, an ugly smile stuck on his face. "We can't keep meeting like this."

"What do you want?" Each syllable is dunked in venom, and I shiver at how hot Sam looks when he's cross.

DeLuca doesn't seem fazed. "Gabriel called. He needs Romano to patrol the south border tonight."

"I'll relay the message," Sam barks.

The nosy jerk doesn't move an inch, and we both glare at him.

He motions to the two of us. "Are you like... taking turns? 'Cause I'd gladly get in line."

"You'd be waiting forever, Perv," I spit out, my pulse swirling.

Sam is shaking from head to toe, and he crouches on all fours. His nails pierce holes in the blanket, the heels of his hands pressing hard into the ground. Energy ripples across his shoulders like he's about to burst into a wolf, his eyes sharp, never leaving DeLuca. "Leave. Now."

The menacing command makes me gulp.

With a snicker, our uninvited guest starts backing away, but he never presents Sam his back until he disappears from view.

"Sam?" I lie down and search the wolf's gaze to reel him back from the brink of his change.

He shakes his head no, and his teeth clank together, goosebumps running along his arms.

Wondering what to do, I bite my bottom lip. The movement captures his attention, his dark eyes now on me. When he gathers the front of my shirt in a fist and dips his head down, I gasp, but he swallows all my sounds into a furious kiss. The back of my head presses into the cool grass below the blanket, my hands flying around Sam's neck.

I sneak a hand below his shirt and trace his shoulder blades. His knee stakes its claim between my legs and rubs against the inside of my thighs. I moan at the delicious contact, breathless. The pointy end of a fang nicks my tongue, and the metallic tang of blood clogs my taste buds.

In a flash, he flips over to his back. His chest rises and falls with shallow breaths. "I'm sorry. I lost control."

I roll to my side and run my fingers up his collarbone through his shirt. "I don't mind." Resting my chin on his chest, I look back to DeLuca's exit path. "That dude is toxic. Have you seen his face, though? He was scared."

"Good. He shouldn't treat you like that." Sam's shoulders wiggle as he shifts into a more comfortable position.

"I'm used to it."

A shadow obscures the wolf's face, and he grazes the arch of my cheekbone to my bottom lip with his thumb. "Do you have fangs?"

I grin and flick the tip of his thumb with my tongue. "Nope."

"So, you never drink blood?"

My nose wrinkles at the notion. Drinking blood is about the only demon thing I hate. "Not often. It tastes weird, but it does help me heal faster."

"Fascinating." He plays with my fingers, looking at my manicured nails. "No claws, either?"

I fumble with the buttons of his shirt, admiring how his muscles strain against the fabric. "Look at you, playing doctor."

He grunts, "Answer the question."

"No claws. I'm ordinary."

It's his turn to crack up. "Oh, I don't think any man would call you ordinary." The intensity burning in his glacial-blue eyes brings a foreign heat to my cheeks, and I have to look away.

It takes a very special man to make a vandella blush.

SECRETS

VICKY

*T*he next day, Dom and I spend a lazy afternoon watching movies on the couch. It's raining cats and wolves outside, drowning out all other sounds until the rumble of an engine is heard. Sam's patients have been coming and going all day, so I don't think much of the sound until the door crashes open, revealing a soaking wet Gabriel.

Dom sits up, untangling himself from me.

The air around the alpha is thick and crackles with pent-up energy, and his murderous glare darkens as it lands on us. In three strides, he's in front of the couch, his clothes dumping half a gallon of water onto the polished hardwood floors. He points a very intimidating finger at Dom. "You fucked her on my desk?"

There's an eerie pause before both their shapes blur, Dom running for his life. The young wolf is fast, but Gabriel is faster and tackles him to the ground. "I'll kill you."

Dom wiggles underneath his alpha's weight and whines.

I can't help but chuckle in delight. "Kill me. It was my idea."

Gabriel growls, "You're next."

The brawl continues and both wolves land a few blows before Dom yields. He apologizes and promises never to "do" me on any surface belonging to Gabriel again. I enjoy every second of the testosterone showdown. If the desk incident taught me anything, it's that Gabriel's hostility is not quite the turn-off I'd wish it to be.

The alpha swipes his forearm across his mouth and stands. "What were you doing in my office?"

Dom rolls to his feet. "Hiding from DeLuca."

Gabriel's brows form a perfect, annoyed line.

"We spied on him," Dom admits.

I smack his shoulder. We promised to keep the secret. He gives me a sheepish grin and shrugs.

Gabriel glowers at each of us in turn. "DeLuca is doing his job better than you are. Leave him alone."

A loud knock interrupts us, and the evidence of Gabriel's temper tantrum vanishes from his body. He misses a step and runs to the front of the house.

His shoulders roll back when he opens the door. "Lena?"

"Hi, sir." The teenager's voice is as squeaky as the tip of her converse on the doormat.

"Is something wrong?"

She looks everywhere but at him, rapping her fingers against her jeans. "No... I have an appointment with Sam."

"Of course. Come in." Gabriel opens the door wide.

Lena waves at me discreetly. "Hi, Vicky."

"Hey."

She nods at Dominic before heading into Sam's office, and I prance into the kitchen for a soda.

Gabriel blocks me with his big arm. "How do you know Lena?"

The quietness of the words gives me pause. "I met her at the grocery store."

He nods impossibly slowly. The hairs at the nape of my neck rise when he leans closer. "Stay away from Lena Dawson."

"What's your problem? I can't talk to anyone while I run around town doing your bidding?"

"You're on thin ice, Blondie. Thin. Ice." With an intimidating growl, he pokes my collarbone.

A loud shout spares me the rest of the lecture. "Gabriel!" The woman from the other day, Billie, bursts into the house. "The north's border been breached. They took John hostage, and Xavier is asking for you. He says he wants to talk."

The scene freezes for a second before Gabriel speaks. "Lena, go home. Sam and Dom, come with me." Gabriel's spine is straight, the calm urgency in his voice strangely soothing. Not one movement is wasted, leaving me no doubt that Gabriel is the best war chief I've ever met.

Sam moves quickly, grabbing a bag from his office.

Dom is already starting the car.

"What can I do?" I ask, eager to help.

"You stay put." The order isn't negotiable, and I know better than to press on.

After they're gone, Lena elbows my side. "You want to follow them?"

I let go of the breath I'd been holding. "Hell, yeah!"

My partner in crime parks her small Toyota in the bushes about two miles down an empty woodsy road. "We'll need to walk the last mile. Thankfully, the wind is with us."

Stilettos and forest hikes aren't exactly compatible, so I pry off my shoes.

"Here." Lena passes me a pair of techy binoculars.

I consider the offering with growing interest. "Wow. Now, I'm curious." Who is she stalking to keep that in her car?

Her ears turn red. "My father is a tracker for the pack. This is his old gear."

Yeah. Okay.

Lena sniffs the air a bunch of times and leads me through the woods. We slow down and crouch for a few hundred feet until she grips my arm. "I hear voices, we can't go any further."

I huff, my supernatural hearing clearly less efficient than hers. "I can't see or hear anything."

"Behind the trees. There." She points to the left, and I look through the binoculars.

A blond man is obscured by a tree, so I only see his right arm and the back of his head. A brunette stands beside him, dressed in a black leather outfit. Leather is so cliché. We can wear pink and still look menacing, can't we?

"Who is she?" I whisper.

"She's Xavier's mate and female alpha to the other pack." Lena's eyes gleam with mischief. "And also Gabriel's ex-wife."

My jaw hangs open.

"It happened like six—seven years ago? When Evelyn left Gabriel for Xavier, it was the talk of the town for—it's still the best gossip around. We all thought Gabriel would hunt her down, but he didn't."

I raise the binoculars to my eyes again. Evelyn is pretty, but she's no match for Gabriel's raw-male magnetism. "I thought you guys mated for life?"

"That's why it's so scandalous. After she left, we found out they never mated. Not properly. Nobody knows why."

So, the blond dude stole his wife but not his mate. While the difference is still unclear to me, it sure looks to mean a lot to them.

I concentrate hard. Their lips are moving but I can't make out the words. "Can you hear what they're saying?"

"A little bit. They're discussing a possible truce."

I frown. "Would that work?"

Lena makes an exaggerated and funny cringe-face. "The dude betrayed him and seduced his wife."

"That's a no."

"A hard no." She looks to the side and wrinkles her nose. "The gusts are uneven. We should go."

Just as she says that, Gabriel turns in our direction, and we both duck behind a fallen tree. A few seconds later, footsteps rustle in our direction. I hold my breath and end up staring straight into the barrel of a gun... and meet Dom's gaze.

Both Lena and I give him a "please don't rat us out" wide-eyed look.

Dom lowers his gun, walking straight past us like we're invisible. Finally, when he's a good twenty feet behind us, he turns back to Gabe and shouts, "It's a couple of squirrels."

He winks on his way back and whispers, "Meet me at DeLuca's in an hour. I have something to show you."

I nod. Sam explained the other day which trail leads to their neighbor's house.

Lena and I hike back to the car, and she drives me home.

"Why are you going to DeLuca's?" she asks.

"We think he wants to cause trouble. He's a creep."

She snorts, "I could have told you that."

"And you? Why did you have an appointment with Sam? Have you been stalking me?" I tease.

A short giggle pops out of her lungs. "Hardly."

She pulls in the driveway, and I slide back into my heels. "Thanks for the ride, Lena."

"It was fun!" Her cheeks are flushed, and her eyes are bright. Her gaze falls to my lips a few times, but I keep my distance.

She's clearly curious, but Gabriel's warning is fresh in my memory, and while I won't be intimidated by anyone, I'd rather not tempt fate.

BAD BOYFRIEND

VICKY

*D*eLuca's house is very similar to the boys' cabin, but smaller. The kitchen lights flood through the huge windows, allowing a wide view of a squeaky-clean interior. I'm leaning behind a large tree trunk, the bark scratching my arms. The thick forest cuts off the setting sun, and I regret not wearing a jacket. Blue and orange stripes are visible above the pointy tips of the pines on the other side of the house. A red pick-up truck and a black luxury car sit in the driveway.

It's silent and boring. Dominic is running abominably late.

My muscles tense when the garage door whines open. DeLuca strolls up to his truck and retrieves a weird electronic device from the back, but I can't quite see what it is. He puts his cell phone to his ear, and his lips starts moving, but I can't hear what he's saying. If only I could get a little closer...

Circling the lot, I tiptoe up the side of the house.

"Sure, boss. I'll meet you there. They have no idea what's coming to them," he says quickly.

The wind shifts abruptly, and I hold my breath. This is bad.

DeLuca's frame appears at the corner, and I flatten myself against a tall bush.

His footsteps get closer and closer until he's towering above me. "Look at that. It's Madonna."

It's too late for a quick escape, so I extricate myself from the branches and dust off my jeans.

"Care to explain why you're here?"

I pry a dry leave from my hair. "I'm a curious person. Like you." *Come on, Dom. Where are you?*

"Let's quench your curious mind." He turns on his heels and returns to his car.

I throw a longing look at the forest but follow him. Why did I come here unarmed? Stupid girl. There's a bunch of wires and duck-taped batteries connected to a multitude of squared shape devices in the back of his truck.

"What are those?" I play naive, but it's pretty clear.

"Bombs." With one quick-as-lightning motion, he grips my hair. My neck screams in pain at the harsh tug, and I try to kick him in the groin.

He sidesteps, my foot scraping his knee instead, and puts his mouth to my ear. "I bet you heard everything I said. Bet you're here to warn them." He frisks my body down with one hand.

A thick tar scent wrinkles my nose. It's pungent and disgusting, gasoline and almonds lingering behind the stink.

"Get your disgusting paws off me!" I scream when his hand reaches my ass.

"I'd fuck you, but the boss frowns upon sexual violence. Though I'm not sure a thing like you can be raped."

I grit my teeth. "We can, asshole. But I'd slice your small cock off before you could find out."

"Big words, there," he says, holding my chin.

I raise a brow. "Try me."

He's freakishly strong, but I give him all I've got and punch his nose with my elbow. I twist around to backstop his knee, sending him flying to the dirt, and run.

A hand stops my escape, and DeNinja immobilizes me in a bear hug. I sink my teeth into his arm, a foul metallic taste making me gag.

He howls and throws a right-hook at my cheek.

I see stars and stagger to keep my balance. A second punch knocks the wind out of me.

DeLuca flings me into the trunk of his black Audi and slams the lid shut. Complete darkness falls over my eyes, my retinas taking a minute to adjust. I punch the back of the seats, but they don't budge. The car's doors open and close a few times before the engine sparks to life.

A cold patch frosts my ribs when DeLuca pulls out of his driveway. Dom won't find me now... I bet DeJerk is working for Xavier and is taking me to him. Whatever they plan to do, it's bad. I need to escape and warn my wolves. I pat around the narrow space for anything I could use as a weapon, but there's nothing.

A few minutes pass before we come to a halt, but the stop is short, and this time, we head out of Wolf Creek. I know because the car remains at full speed in a single direction for more than ten minutes, and no road around town is that straight, so we must be on the highway. When we slow down again, a few abrupt changes in direction cause me to knock my head against the bulge of the wheel.

A garage door opens loudly, and we come to a stop.

"Where's Dominic?"

My heart skips a beat, and my eyes widen at the sound of Gabriel's voice.

"I couldn't find him. But I found *this* in my bushes. She heard our conversation." DeLuca opens the trunk and throws me to the ground at Gabriel's feet.

The alpha kneels next to me and wraps a hand in my hair, angling my face to him. "Not a spy, eh? I should have known better."

Disappointment drags down every syllable before he releases me and stands back up, turning to his lackey. "Gather the others. We need to act now."

With a wicked smile, DeLuca hops back into his car and drives off.

Gabriel clicks the garage door closed. "You tell me everything right now, and I'll kill you quickly." He walks in circles around me.

I shuffle to my ass, my legs folded beneath me, my stunned silence only pissing Gabriel off further.

He points a gun at my face. "How about I help you out? Evelyn sent you to spy on me."

"Why would your ex-wife send me?" I croak, warming my throat back into working order.

"Because you're exactly—" His nostrils flare. "How else would you know her name?"

"Lena gave me the cliff notes of your family scandal earlier," I explain slowly. I need to buy time.

The safety clicks off. "I told you to stay away from Lena."

"Relax, nothing happened." I glance around the industrial storage facility. "Where are we?"

"Your employer's weapon depot. I've been searching for it for a year. Xavier made a big mistake this time."

I raise a brow, considering the loot with new eyes. "Are we going to steal their stuff?"

Gabriel slides a huge metal crate closer to me with one arm, his muscles straining at the effort. "Stop saying we."

"I'm not a spy. I was in DeLuca's bushes because I thought he was making a move against you. Are you sure he's on your side?"

"100%." He tucks the gun back into its holster and drags me from the concrete floor to the crate. "Sit. Now, I'll be asking the questions. Why bring vampires into this? To throw me off Evelyn's scent and make your story believable? Was she hoping I'd get distracted?" He reaches inside his pocket and snaps his pocket-knife open.

Saliva burns like acid down my throat. "Are you going to torture me?"

There's a definite pause. "Maybe."

"Liar. I can see it in your eyes. You won't hurt me." I try the words on for size, hoping they're true.

A dark glint shimmers in his gray eyes. "How about I leave you here and blow this whole place up?"

I press my lips together. He won't torture me, but he'll kill me. And I'm not sure I can talk him out of it.

Tires screech in the distance, and Gabriel's body stiffens to the point of immobility. "You found a way to alert them."

"I did no such thing." I search his gaze to make him believe me.

Gabriel flattens himself to the thick concrete wall and sneaks a glance through the small squared window next to the garage door. He flips off a big electronic switch and pushes a crate to cover the window.

Car doors open and shut in rapid succession while I keep count. "Alpha or no alpha, there's at least six of them out there."

"Seven with you," he says wryly.

Loud curses resonate from outside.

Adrenaline whips my pulse into a frenzy when gunshots ricochet off the garage door. "I'm on your side, you fool. I can help you."

"Dream on, Blondie." His hand closes around my throat.

I grip his fingers. "What choice do you have? If I'm with them, you're toast anyway. Is it so important that I die? Take a chance on me. I can stall them." The dry, metallic sound of a saw scratches at my ears, and the floor of the storage unit starts to vibrate. Whoever is on the other side is cutting a path forward, and there's clearly no other way in or out of here. "Please, Gabriel. I'm not your enemy."

With a roar, he lets me go.

I tear my dress off, keeping my hot pink thong and matching bra on. "Bite me."

He scowls, unmoving. "What?"

"Bite my neck. As hard as you can. Now!" I grab a fistful of his black hair and bring his mouth to my pulse point. My eyes screw shut. Gabe follows my command, his teeth tearing through the flesh like I'm a nice fluffy cupcake. Hot blood trickles down the slope of my neck to my shoulder and splashes across my chest.

He holds me to him, frozen for a second, and his arms shake.

A hot shudder slices through my body as he licks the wound clean with his tongue, a pained growl rumbling in his chest.

"Find a good spot to shoot from." I push him off, and he staggers backwards.

Red drops glisten on his lips before he wipes his mouth off with his sleeve. "What are you going to do?"

"What I do best. Distract." I fluff my hair, smudge a bit of blood across my naked stomach, and sit back down with my legs crossed. My palms are braced behind me, holding me halfway up.

An almost naked, bloody vandella sprawled on an army-sized crate of weapons... If that doesn't get their attention, nothing will.

A rectangle is slowly carved into the garage door, sparks of hot metal spraying into the air. When it's large enough for a human to walk through, a big hand peels the passageway open.

Six silhouettes stream through in a blur. The wolves pause and sniff the air, their weapons searching for a target. They are all wearing Kevlar vest.

Evelyn is the first to speak. "Where is Gabriel?"

Three guns are aimed at little old *moi*, but I don't budge. Prey show fear. Predators smile. "You're too late. He's gone. When he realized you were coming, he left me here as a diversion so you wouldn't run after him."

When you're bluffing your heart out, always stick to the closest version of the truth. They clearly have a spy in-house, probably DeLuca, which means the cavalry is not coming. We'll have to kill them ourselves.

The tallest of the five men prowls forward, assessing me with a serious glare that doesn't quite mask his interest. All-American build.

Handsome face. Impressive muscles. But he pales in comparison to Gabriel.

"So, you're the other Alpha." I lick my lips. "I've developed quite a taste for the rush." I stand up slowly, watching their reactions. They do not clasp their guns tighter or raise their swords higher, so I prance closer to them. I focus my gaze on the alpha, hoping two things will happen. One. He'll decide he needs to fuck me. Two. Evelyn will get jealous and stupid. "I could help you kill him. He was holding me captive, you know."

Xavier motions to his men to lower their guns and rests the tip of his sword on the ground. "We know."

I angle the bite on my neck to Evelyn for a split second.

Blood drains from her face. "He bit you?"

I shrug like it means nothing to me. "He's kinky."

"Gabriel has never marked a woman before. Why you?" Xavier asks.

I rap my fingers against his large arm, dosing my powers in small amounts not to spook him, gradually increasing the pull until his pupils are all black. "Why don't you try me and find out?"

Xavier grins. "Dex, Spike. You patrol the surrounding woods and make sure it's not an ambush. Grant, Kyle, you check that Gabriel didn't tamper with anything in here. We can't afford to lose these." With shallow breaths, he inches closer to me. "Call the others. We have to move everything out before they attack."

His wolves look between the two of us but eventually follow his orders.

"You're not seriously thinking we can trust her?" Evelyn whispers under her breath, clearly shaken.

"I have no intention of *trusting* her. Get to work, Lyn." Xavier's hand closes around my arm, and he pulls me outside.

He flattens me against the side of the building and licks the blood off my neck.

Clearly, my powers work better on him than on Gabriel. For an alpha, I'm disappointed in the slow trickle of energy coming from him. Gabriel packs more in a glare than this guy does in a full-blown kiss. My plan to feed off him to juice my powers is dead in the water.

The heavy taste of coffee clogs my tongue, but I kiss him back. He's not half bad. Nice technique, a good dose of urgency. A sizable bulge in his pants.

"We heard about you, but I didn't quite believe the reports." An arm drapes around me, and he strokes my back up and down.

"Did they do me justice?"

"Not at all."

He clearly doesn't plan on assaulting me or anything, which gives me a little time to think.

Once he's naked, I could probably knee his junk and run off, but that won't help Gabriel, and they'll chase after me. No, my best bet is probably to play this all the way and hope Gabriel has the sense to remain hidden. Who knows, I might get to play the double agent if they don't kill me.

Xavier snakes a hand inside my underwear.

The tight knot in my stomach stings with fresh bile. Maybe there's another way to stall him. "Won't your mate mind?" I backtrack.

"She does not own me. I've heard about your kind... You're a good little slut, aren't you?"

Ooooh, this guy is going to die young. I plaster a fake smile on my lips and wink. "The best."

With a frown, he grazes my sex, and I'm itching to knee his junk after all.

"You do not smell like him down there," he says.

I plant my lips on his before he realizes that I've lied. His shoulders relax, his hand leaving the confines of my underwear to cup my breasts over the pink lace.

Two black vans pull up, more wolves spilling to the curb, but since Xavier is still kissing me, they're not the help I'd hoped for. At this rate, they'll soon find Gabriel in there.

Engines roar up the road again, and this time, Xavier's head whips up to face the noise. Three red pick-up trucks are racing toward us.

Gunshots thunder from inside the weapon depot.

Sam erupts from one of the trucks, his gun raised straight at us. His aim waivers when he takes in the sight before him, and deep lines form at the corner of his expressive blue eyes.

Betrayal renders his face totally unrecognizable, a deep pain written across his features. His jaw is clenched harder than I've ever seen it, and he shoots at Xavier.

The rogue alpha uses me as a shield. Two silver rounds bite my flesh, and hot blood pours against my fingers. Fantastic. If I were a shifter, I'd be dead.

Wolves and soldiers blur from all sides as I fall to my back on the gravel, the smell of slaked lime and mortar tightening my throat. The sky is heavy with stars, quickly eclipsed by Sam's ashen features.

Blood smears on his face when I cup his cheek with a shaky hand. "You shot me."

NOTHING FAILS

VICKY

A machine grumbles next to me as I wake up. I'm in Dominic's bed, fluids hooked to my right arm. Fresh pain radiates in my belly at the first shift. I pull the black t-shirt up my stomach and look down at the gunshot wounds. The red holes are neatly closed, so Sam probably patched me up.

The stitches are rough to the touch.

DeLuca walks by the open door, and my pulse quickens. His eyes rove over me with barely-contained glee. "No hard feelings?"

Slime glues the words together, making this a total non-apology, and acid rises to my mouth.

Dom's large frame obscures the threshold. "She needs rest. Go home, DeLuca."

I relax against the pillow. "What happened? Is everyone alright?"

Dom sits at the edge of the bed. "We won. Blew the weapons to pieces. It was quite a show. They had serious army gear in there, enough to take the whole town out. We lost two wolves, though, and

Gabriel was shot, too. He told us what you did." His warm hands closes around my fingers.

"I can't believe I passed out." I shift on the bed and fumble with the IV line, itching to tear it from my arm.

"I can't believe Sam shot you," Dom says on a cringe. "I'm so sorry for leaving you out there alone. I was cornered by Lena's father. He was worried that you were trying to seduce his daughter."

Sam thunders into the room, his white coat streaked with blood. "Feeling nauseous?" He plops a digital thermometer in my mouth.

"No," I mumble.

In full physician mode, he looks at the numbers on the fluid pump. The thermometer beeps, and he picks it up before flashing a light in both my eyes. "At the rate you're healing, two days of rest, and you should be good as new." His movements are very methodical. Adjusting my IV, checking my stitches, taking my blood pressure.

Where are we on my *I'm-sorry-for-riddling-you-with-bullets* order? The doctor thoroughly avoids my glare.

"Dom, can you give us a moment?" I ask.

"Sure." He squeezes my hand before walking out.

"You're acting weird." He doesn't slow-down. "It's because you caught me with the other alpha, isn't it?"

His fists clench.

"It didn't mean anything. I had to run interference."

"How is kissing me any different?" His previously dispassionate tone is crackling with hurt, like glass breaking after impact.

I blink once. Twice. "Because it is."

"And I have to take your word on it? Because you say so?"

My voice raises, my patience getting thinner and thinner on the account of the holes in my stomach. "No. Because you feel it. Why would I stay if I didn't like you and Dom? Why would I care about your twisted politics?"

His stare is glued to the wall behind me. "It's convenient to hide here. Hiding from vampires on our land is the safest bet there is."

"Is that really what you think?" This rotten replacement of the sweet apology I had envisioned turns my stomach. "Is that why you shot me?"

The storm in his blue eyes is blinding, his entire body shaking. "I aimed for him! I never thought he'd use you as a shield."

"You clearly thought I'd betrayed you."

Sitting next to me in a blur, he snatches my hand and pulls it to his mouth desperately. "Not *betrayed*. I thought you'd been playing us all along. I mean—I should have trusted my instincts. I should have trusted *you*. But I felt so played, so angry." Hot lips press against my knuckles. "Damn it I—I'm falling for you, Vicky. When I saw you with him, it felt like my heart had been ripped out of my chest. I can't believe I pulled that trigger."

I tangle my fingers in his curls, my chest warm and my throat tight. "Hey, it's okay."

He's man-crying now, choking on every other breath not to let actual tears through. "It's not. I shot you. I almost killed you."

"You didn't. I'm tougher than I look."

He hides his face in my neck, his arms draped around me, and gently pulls me to him. "I'll never hurt you again. Never."

I pat his back. "Shh. It'll be okay."

SAM DOESN'T LET me out of his sight for the next two days. He feeds me kisses and sandwiches *à la Dom*, and we shack up in his room, watching movies and each other. I know he's partly doing it out of guilt, but I love the attention. His bedroom in the opposite of Dom's. It's clean, for starters. The bright blue paint makes it feel bigger. Dom has a king-sized bed, but Sam has a double, and the rest of the space is occupied by a large desk. It's cluttered with papers and books, but there's no clothes or shoes lying around.

"What's going to happen now?" I ask, a big piece of red liquorice in my mouth.

"Since Xavier escaped, they are preparing for a retaliatory attack.

Werewolves heal from most wounds in 72 hours, so it should be soon."

A shiver quakes my body. "Is that why Dom spent the night out and why Gabriel hasn't come to see me yet?"

"They're busy. I volunteered to stay with you and prepare the house in case we have a lot of wounded."

I swallow hard and sink into the mattress. Wounded. Deaths. "I want to help. I'll fight with you."

"Don't be ridiculous."

My eyes narrow. "I got unlucky back there with the fainting. Unless there's aconite involved, I'm pretty strong. And always underestimated."

"You have to rest for another couple of days. Doctor's orders." He descends upon me, and my lips part, welcoming him.

There's been a real shift in Sam since the *accident*. He doesn't hold back as much. His tongue is more assertive, his hands more adventurous. Maybe it has to do with him trusting me more, or maybe he's coming to terms with his feelings.

I run my fingers through his hair. "You know... I'm going to need more than kisses soon." I watch his face, hoping he'll volunteer.

A dark glower is all I get. "I just removed your stitches."

"Biology doesn't care about doctor's orders."

He balls my hands in his and kisses them. "Can't you wait a bit longer?"

"No," I answer honestly. The hunger has grown all day from a nip to a painful pressure. The kisses stopped soothing the ache a few hours ago, now only adding fuel to the fire. Each brush of Sam's tongue sinks directly to the place deep inside my belly that howls for his cock. And the beast his getting louder and louder.

He nods slowly and stands up, giving me free rein. He might be ready for make-out sessions, but he's not ready for more.

I wander into the kitchen, pretty sure I heard the porch's door swing open not too long ago.

The scents of coffee beans and peanut butter linger into the air, the midday sun streaming through the windows. The loud rumbles of the air conditioning scratch at my ears.

Dominic is leaning against the island, facing me. "Morning." He sips his coffee.

"It's one o'clock."

"Afternoon, then." A lazy grin spreads on his lips, and my stomach tightens. It's only been two days, but I missed him. Missed his rough touch, his unapologetic kisses, and his infectious laughter.

Standing on my tiptoes, I wrap my arms around his neck.

He breathes me in and presses his forehead to mine. "God. Sam has to stop hogging you."

"I'll tell him you said so." I hike his shirt up and roam the sinews of his chest. He smells like the grass he just cut, and his white shirt is peppered with greens strands. "I'm hungry."

A gentle hand slides under the hem of my dress and caresses the small of my back. "He still won't touch you, then."

"Look at you, wanting all the details." I don't mind that Sam wants to wait anymore. It's...new. And hot. And it does all sort of twisted things to my heart. But I still need Dom's uncomplicated and delicious sex drive.

What can I say? I'm greedy.

Dom picks me up and deposits me on the island. I spread my legs on each side of his waist.

He peels my cotton dress off, and his fingers tremble over the faded red scars on my abdomen. "I still can't believe he shot you."

"Me neither."

"He'll grovel for months, at least."

"Now, I can get on board with that." A big grin splits my face at the image of a Sam-slave, doing my bidding to earn my forgiveness. Preferably a naked one.

I place an open-mouthed kiss on the side of Dominic's face while he strips. I've been running on just kisses for too long, and my stomach cramps with need. I shift my butt closer to the edge of the island and lean back on my elbows.

"Careful, you're still hurt."

I love how protective he gets.

Leaning over me, he sucks my breast into his mouth and licks the nipple, nibbling the rosy flesh until I'm out of breath. He teases the other with his thumb, flicking the peak so hard that I gasp. I squeeze his hips with my thighs. "Please, Dom."

"I missed them. Give us a minute."

I glance down and smirk at how entranced he looks. "I'm sorry. Am I interrupting?"

"Kind of." He doubles his efforts on the other side.

I chuckle and arch into him, the sensation melting me into butter.

Dom works his cock out of his pants with one hand and explores my folds with the other. "Fuck, baby. You're so ready for me." With a hiss, he impales me on his long, hot erection.

Hallelujah.

I draw a long breath, resting my head on the island for a second, reveling in the feel of him tucked deep inside me. His hips find a gentle rhythm, but I'm not in the mood for a healthy meal. I want a red steak and fries.

I sit-up, masking a wince, and slap his ass. "Don't hold out on me, wolf."

I let my lure build and feed it to him in waves. A groan falls through his lips, his hips now insatiable.

A thin film of sweat gathers on his chest.

Then, I meet Sam's eyes across the room. A hot flash sears through my stomach, and I sink my nails in Dom's shoulder blade. "Harder."

Each thrust drags along my g-spot, and my gaze is still locked with Sam's.

"Sam is watching," I whisper into Dom's ear.

He palms my ass, kneading the flesh. "Good."

I come undone in Dom's arms, the pleasure so quick and violent it rips a cry from me.

Sam holds my stare for a second before vanishing.

Dom is on the crest of his orgasm, too. He forgets to be careful and grips my waist, riding me deep until I come again. We both fall over the edge, grasping and groping at each other. His hot pants heat up my neck, my brain in mush at the pleasure radiating from my over-sensitive sex.

My wound tickles and heals because of Dom's energy.

I realize then what I really want. Both of them. But Saint Sam will never go for that... right?

Dom meets my gaze, and it's like he can read my thoughts because a wicked smile spreads on his lips. He glances to where Sam was a second ago. "Don't worry, it won't be long now. He's spiraling."

I smother a giggle in his neck. "And that's good?"

"Fucking A. We were in a rut before you showed up."

"Rut or routine?" I tease him.

"Rut. I'm talking sleep-till-noon, eat-nothing-but-cereal, no-show-ering-for-a-week and passing out in front of *Naked and Afraid* rut. It was ugly."

"*Naked and Afraid?*"

"It cracks us up. Humans are so whiny."

A full-bellied laugh quakes my body. "You're a peculiar man, Dominic Romano."

He licks the side of my face affectionately, tasting my skin in a way that reminds me of his animal nature. "And you're fucking perfect."

And for the first time in a while—maybe the first time in my entire life—I feel perfect.

BLUE JEANS

VICKY

*D*om catches the hilt of a long sword in mid-air.

"Show off," I say.

We're hanging out in the living room, waiting for Gabriel. Dom is doing acrobatics with his sword to both impress me and kill time while Sam inventories his medical supplies. The alpha spent the night barricaded in his office. DeLuca came and went at dawn, but other than that, he refused to see anyone.

"Are you two ready?" Gabriel barks as he finally graces us with his presence. I've only caught a glance of him since our peculiar bonding experience at the weapon depot, and my mouth is dry.

My wolves both hop to their feet and nod, their backs stiff as though they're soldiers heading for war, which I guess is true enough.

Gabe's dark gaze lands on me. "What are you wearing?"

I look down at my sneakers and black sports pants. It's not sexy or provocative at all, and I raise a brow. "Dom told me you were heading for the north border, expecting a big showdown. I'm coming with you."

"No," the alpha grunts.

I cross my arms. "Should I wait to see who wins and throw whoever comes through the doors a party?"

Gabe hooks his gun holster over his shoulder. "We'll win."

"What if you don't?" I ask flippantly.

A low growl passes through his tight lips. "Dom, you can't keep telling your girlfriend classified information."

Dominic stops twirling his sword around his wrist long enough to glance at us. "She wants to help."

Gabriel snatches his cell from his pocket, and his scold loosens. He walks towards the front door, his thumbs flying over the screen. "Fine. Take her with you then."

I frown. Something isn't right.

Gabriel waves us off before heading outside. "I'll take my truck and meet you there."

Dom points to the office. "You'll need a sword, too. They're in Gabe's office."

With a victorious grin, I open the door. A mahogany desk and computer chair are facing the window to my left, and a table is leaning against the wall in front of me. Three swords hang on the wall, six of them missing from the display. The table underneath is cluttered with all the pointy and deadly gear to make a girl happy. The whole room smells like the ocean, and I breathe in deep.

The other day, I left the house without a weapon. That was a big mistake. I tuck a sheathed dagger in my bra, a gun with silver bullets at my back, and pick up the longest sword. Those wolves won't know what hit them, and Gabe can grovel at my feet after I save the day.

The ergonomic leather chair by Gabriel's desk is glossy under the sun. The map sprawled on the desk catches my eye, and I snoop in Gabriel's paperwork. There's a big red circle around an area called *Dustin SQ,* and the borders to the shifters' land are marked with thick black lines. A smaller piece of paper sticks out from underneath, and I discreetly inch it down.

It's an aerial view of a huge sand quarry. Red lines are drawn around a central pit, dots set at regular intervals. *11:00 am* has been written with the same pen, and I glance at the clock. It's 10:30.

Gabriel doesn't mind me going with Dominic. Why? Maybe because he's going somewhere else.

I run back to Dom. My mouth hangs open, and I consider telling him the truth, but I can't take the risk that I'm wrong. I'm not as crucial to this fight as Dominic and Sam. If I rope them into going with me to this red circle thing and we end up miles from the action, they'll hate me. "I changed my mind. I'm staying here."

Dom's frown is worth a thousand words. "You're kidding."

"Go!" I wave my wolves off.

"What's going on?" Sam asks, hovering in the doorway.

I meet each of their gaze in turn. "I can't explain now. Just go."

"But—" Sam starts.

I push Dom toward the door. "You're wasting time."

They exchange a confused glance but hurry out.

I grab the keys to Sam's Jeep and clasp them in my hands.

I have to see this hunch through. Why would Gabriel confer only with DeLuca if he didn't have a crazy plan? I can't shake the feeling that he's walking right into a trap.

The mysterious quarry is right on the southern edge of town. Deep down, I hope I'm wrong and that Gabriel is with the guys. When a big steel fence marking the entrance of the quarry comes into view, my pulse surges. It's open, and I speed up past the empty gate. My hands clench around the steering wheel as I park right beside Gabriel's black truck.

He came here instead. Why?

The alpha is standing atop a tall dune, looking through binoculars. His leather jacket flaps in the wind when he turns to face me, and I climb the ridge of sand hurriedly.

"You're not supposed to be here." He cranes his neck around to the cars. "You came alone, right?"

"Yes." I observe the expanse of sand. It's desolate. Beautiful in its silent emptiness, like a graveyard. "Where did you send the others?"

"They're right where I want them, stalling Evelyn." He tosses his binoculars to the ground. "I asked Xavier to meet me here."

The too-cool-for-school attitude boils my blood. "Alone? Why?"

Gabriel starts heading downhill and away from the entrance. "Because this war needs to end. Xavier was counting on the weapons we blew up to overpower us. Now, he's vulnerable, but his hurt pride is calling for blood. It's the perfect time to strike." He pauses halfway down. "You should go back to the house. You're going to ruin my plan."

I follow in his wake, my feet slipping against the sand. "I saved your ass the other day."

Gabe clicks his tongue. "You humiliated him. He's gunning for you. If something goes wrong, you could get killed." He's not saying the words in a protective manner, but in warning. That way, he can't be held accountable for it if it happens.

My grip tightens on the hilt of my sword. "I can take care of myself. In fact, I bet that I can slice more necks than you."

Gabe shakes his head like I'm missing the entire point. "There's only one neck that matters. His wolves shouldn't be punished for his sins."

My heart melts while my brain rings in alarm. I didn't take Gabriel for the classic storybook hero that would risk his life for honor. "Is that why you're walking right into an ambush?"

He averts his gaze. "There's only one way to end this without a bloodbath."

Adrenaline rushes through my veins. He's crazy. "Xavier won't go for a duel. I've known him five seconds, and I know that."

"So do I."

"I'm lost." If Xavier won't go for a duel, what is he hoping to achieve here?

He wets his lips. "It's about respect. His wolves will doubt him for refusing to fight me. They'll realize his strength lies in numbers, numbers that he ripped right from the human world and transformed into soldiers."

"They follow him of their own free will, no?" I ask.

His closes his eyes for a second. "What choice do they have? Do you know how hard it is for a newly bitten wolf to refuse a direct order from his alpha? Almost impossible. He wrecked their lives and forced them to fight for him. I bet they're angry." He pries his phone from his pocket and raises it to his ear. "Yes?"

Dom's voice barrels through the line, loud enough for me to hear. "Where are you, boss?"

"Don't bother with that. Is Evelyn there?" Gabe asks.

"Yes," Dom answers.

"Good. Keep an eye on her." The alpha hangs up.

I look around us to the barren landscape and play nervously with my fingers. "Why didn't you take Dom with you?"

"Xavier is not stupid. Evelyn is reporting that Dom and Sam are over there as we speak. In fact, she probably checked that all the warriors are over there before giving the okay."

I nudge his hip with my own. "You're lucky I'm nosy because this is going to get ugly."

His lips twitch.

We slide across another tall mound, and the deep pit in front of us rings a bell. It's the one that was marked on the map, its slight teardrop shape unmistakable. As we reach the middle of the barren quarry, four man-shaped silhouettes rise from the hill in front of us, and the clicks of guns resonate across the sand.

Three wolves growl from the surrounding dunes, and Xavier slides a few feet closer to us.

Eight against two. How is this fight going to end well?

Xavier points to me. "You call that backup?"

"I wanted to come alone, but she's pig-headed." Gabriel throws his gun to the ground, and it digs into the sand with a faint *whoosh*.

"No weapons. You and me. We end this now. No one else has to get hurt."

Xavier smirks. "Why would I agree to that? I have you right where I want you."

"So, you refuse?" Gabriel's gaze travels from one wolf to the other, his steady, commanding voice echoing around the dunes.

Xavier starts shooting.

Gabriel sidesteps, avoiding the bullets.

The wolves jolt into action, leaping down the steep slopes like they have skis instead of paws.

Gabriel digs a hand into his jeans' pockets, pries out a small black device, and presses a button.

The mountains around us explode into huge clouds of dust and fire. The sand scratches my skin on its way down, filling my mouth and ears and blinding me to anything that's not in close proximity. I hear howls and screams of pain.

When the dust clears, I see that three wolves have bit the dust, their bodies half buried, their paws still struggling to grip the shifting sand.

Xavier claws himself out of a sand hole at the bottom of the mountain, his nostrils flaring.

I watch, mesmerized, as Gabriel launches himself at the other alpha, each movement brimming with power, no step wasted or unsure. He's a sight to watch, and my mind flashes back to my childhood when Simba fought Scar. Two muscular human-shaped wolves collide with each other.

I can't look away, and I realize the others—men and wolves—can't either. We're all standing there, transfixed by what's happening, until one wolf finally slithers in my direction, his teeth bared. I grab the gun at my back and shoot him, the bullet lodging in his shoulder. He falls to his side with a whine.

I duck to avoid a gunshot, the air whizzing two inches above my head, and a second wolf takes advantage of the situation to tackle me down. We wrestle in the sand, my powers useless against an animal.

The white wolf snaps his big, pointy teeth an inch from my throat, and I sink my fingers in his eye sockets, holding his jaw back with my other hand.

A guttural roar calls my attention back to the fight.

Gabriel rips Xavier's head off with his bare hands, and a deafening silence falls over the quarry. Blood splashes everywhere and mixes with the sand, forming red mud at the alpha's feet.

The wolf below me struggles to free himself, and I let him go.

Gabriel swipes his wrist across his mouth and drops the body of his opponent. "Listen to me. What your alpha never mentioned is that you're all welcome to join us. As long as you're willing to follow the rules."

One of the men staggers to his feet and takes a step forward. "Your rules."

"Yes, my rules. I've been around long enough to know what works. Now, run off and tell the others that the war is over. Xavier is dead. I'll welcome any wolf who wants to join my pack with open arms, but they'll need to pledge their allegiance to me *and* to the rules."

A bad bruise is blossoming on his jaw, his shirt drenched in sweat and blood, but the sum of it all only enhances his violent beauty. He's so charismatic in that moment, his muscles bunched tight as he towers over his kill, his chest heaving. The wolf is present in every breath, every shift, every stare he deals out in turn so that every single one of us is slashed by the intensity and power behind his piercing gray eyes.

"I'll be expecting the ones interested at the north border Friday at dusk." Gabriel turns on his heels and starts walking back towards the cars.

The wolves look stunned.

The farthest of the two human-shaped men shouts, "Friday's the full moon. Many of us will need to... run."

Gabriel smirks. "I know. Come to me, and I'll show you how a real pack runs."

I catch up with him, his silhouette already disappearing behind the first dune. "How can you be so confident that they won't regroup and attack? Couldn't they pick another leader?"

"Packs without alphas are doomed to fail, and to be one, you need more power and experience than any of them has. Even Evelyn is far from being alpha-material, and Xavier was barely worthy of the name."

I'd pledge my life to Gabriel in a heartbeat if I was them. Hell, I'm so star-struck, I have to hold back my powers two-fold not to embarrass myself. "Still, they're human, too. They might want to get even. What if Evelyn wants revenge?" My eyes narrow. "Do you plan on welcoming her back with open arms?"

The possibility is so vile that acid rises to my mouth.

Gabriel's jaw ticks. "If Evelyn wants to live, she'll disappear."

The answer brings a shiver to my core, and I miss a step. "I must admit; your plan was smart and efficient."

The praise coaxes a tiny smile out of Gabriel. "Was that a compliment?"

"Why did you keep it a secret from the guys?" I ask, sidestepping his ego-stroking question.

His expression darkens. "There's a mole in my close circle. You weren't wrong about that, but it's not DeLuca."

"The man is horrid."

"Perhaps, but he's loyal. I don't have to be friends with all my wolves. They just have to obey. Friends are more likely to betray you anyway."

The dire undertone of that last part makes me pause.

"You don't think Sam or Dom..."

"I don't know. I was wrong about you, and I want to believe it's not them, but I can't be sure. Xavier learned things only someone very close to me would know. He had my exact schedule, learned about your existence in record time, and alerted them that we were alone at the weapon depot." His gaze weights heavily on me. "How did you end up at DeLuca's the other night?"

My throat itches. "Dom told me to meet him there, but he didn't show..."

"My current theory is that the mole was also there at DeLuca's, saw him take you, followed his car to the depot, and called it in. They were probably hoping I'd be too busy killing or fucking you to hear them coming. If it's the kid..." Gabriel trails off, his voice cracking at the end.

"It's not Dom." The words are steady because I believe them.

"You really trust him? I've known him for ten years and I'm not sure." He rolls his eyes. "Don't tell me you're falling for him."

"Are you jealous?" I chime.

Gabriel snorts. "You wake up in a strange house, fuck the first guy you see and end up with a ring on your finger? That doesn't happen. I don't believe in fate."

"Me neither. It's not about fate." Our eyes lock.

"Then what is it about?" The cynicism in his voice is thick.

"Dumb luck." I press my tongue to the back of my front teeth.

Humor shines in his eyes, and he laughs. It's a full-bodied laugh, his smile showing off his perfect white teeth, his face relaxed and open. The change is glaring, unexpected, and I can't look away. A weird pride flutters in my chest that I erased his quasi-permanent frown. My insides are all mushy, the dazzling chuckles deep and hypnotic.

There's something both new and ancient about him. It's electrifying.

"Now, I have to rely on dumb luck to be happy?" he yanks the Jeep's door open for me.

I stay with both feet firmly planted on the ground and look up at him. "Why did you bite them—Sam and Dom."

He raises a cocky brow. "Changing the subject? Are you admitting you have no arguments left?"

"Humor me."

His arm is still braced against the opened door, hovering above me, the muscles tight like he can't make up his mind about what to do with it. The wind plays with his black hair, the usually neat spikes all disheveled. His dark stubble is peppered with blood. Sweat and sand formed a few crusty islands on his neck, and I curl my hands into fists not to reach for them.

He studies me for the longest time, his enigmatic gaze rippling against my cheeks. "Sam was fatally injured a few days before the end of the war. He was the best and most generous soldier I knew. I couldn't let his story end like that. Dom was a kid caught in the wrong place at the wrong time, stabbed in a New York subway for chop change..."

A lock of hair obscures my face at a sudden burst of wind, and I hold my breath when Gabriel's hand finally leaves the car door, his gaze fixed on it. Just as I'm sure he's about to tuck it back behind my ear, he makes a fist and lets his arm fall at his side.

My heart pulses in my throat. "You saved them."

He buries his hands in his jacket. "I cursed them. Sure, they were going to die anyway, so they didn't mind as much, but the life of a bitten wolf isn't all rosy, either. Sam and I spent three years in France taming his beast. Dom was luckier, but this town is too small for him and always will be. That was Xavier's mistake. When you think all humans would die to be like us, you end up with resentful wolves. Never mind the fact that they don't all make it through the change."

I hop on the driver seat. "You could have been assigned to another unit or chosen a different subway stop. Dumb luck changed your life forever too. For the better."

He considers my statement carefully, his gray eyes softer than I've ever seen them. "You're not wrong, Blondie. Not wrong at all."

SOMEWHERE ONLY WE KNOW

SAM

"*J* can't believe you got to see it all while Dom and I waited like useless pawns." My arms are wrapped around my girl, our bodies entangled on the living room L-shaped couch.

Her lips graze my ear. "What happened on your side?"

"Evelyn talked our ears off until the wolves you let loose came running. She howled so loud when they told her Xavier was dead... It was almost sad." I blow softly on her neck, and she relaxes against my chest. I can't believe she forgave me for shooting her. I'll make it up to her. I'll spend the rest of my life trying if I have to.

"That's nice," she says on a sigh. "Will a lot of wolves join your ranks, you think?"

"Probably. It's scary to be without an alpha. We'll know soon enough. The full moon is only two nights away. " Kissing her neck, I study her breaths, the tiny changes in her gait, and the subtle richness of her moans. I'm trying to distinguish between what she needs and what she wants. To Dom, the two are one and the same. For me, it's all the difference in the world. She feeds on the desire she incites in us, but she's not reduced to her hunger the same way I'm not defined by my need for fresh meat. She must also lust for sex besides her need to feed.

A lazy grin spreads on her candy-red lips. "You're still studying me. Why are you so sure it's not magic?"

"Our bodies are not entirely human, but we still work the same. We need food, shelter, sex... We also want safety, intimacy." Love. I get the feeling my alluring sex goddess hasn't been loved in too long.

"Are you admitting you need sex too?" She says in jest.

She watches me intently, her irises twinkling with mischief. They go from a very human blue when she's just fed to full-on purple when she's hungry or using her powers. Now, they're dangerously close to purple, and I know it won't be long before her body heats up and eats away at my sanity. A part of me is ready to give in, dying to make her feel good and fulfill her needs, desperate to leap into this connection that grows stronger by the day.

But most of me is still too raw, and a little fragment of my soul will probably always feel guilty.

I never consciously decided that I would remain faithful to my late wife. But somehow, I did.

And now it's been so long that it feels weird to—not.

I clear my throat. "After... I mean—I got used to not having it, I guess."

"Who was she?" There's no guile or jealousy in the question. Just patience and curiosity.

My throat doesn't clamp shut, and I say her name out loud for what feels like the first time in forever. "My late wife, Sybil. We were together for forty years. I married her before the change."

Vicky twines our fingers. "I'm sorry. I can't even comprehend how much you miss her."

"I do miss her. I'll always miss her." There's an empty space in my chest where her laughs used to echo. I don't cry anymore, not often anyway, but it doesn't mean I don't miss her. "Maybe I'm afraid that heaven exists, and that she'll be disappointed in me. Maybe I know she'd understand, and I'm using her as an excuse."

Sometimes I hate that I studied psychology. I'd rather stay in the dark than look at the truth. It's not only about faithfulness and the fear that loving another means forgetting her. I'm afraid for myself. Losing Sybil was the worst kind of heartbreak, and I don't want to go through that pain again.

"Remember when you asked why I didn't live in town?" I trail my lips along Vicky's pulse point. "After Gabriel bit me, we spent three years in Europe. I couldn't take the chance of boarding a boat to America. It was three difficult years, away from my wife, my family, my whole world, but it was nothing compared to the war.

"When we came back, Gabriel brought me to this town and allowed Sybil to come and live with me, but she didn't feel comfortable here. She was too freaked out by the whole werewolf thing, but she loved me, so we compromised. We moved back to the East coast, and I went back to school and got my Ph.D. She was happier there, but I wasn't. I missed running with the pack. I missed Gabriel and the sense of belonging, but I felt I owed it to her to live as though I was the human she'd married."

"She never considered becoming like you?" Vicky asks softly.

"We talked about it. The odds of surviving the first change are pretty good, though not absolute, but she couldn't come to terms with becoming one of us. We chose not to have kids, knowing my altered genes would most likely be passed on to our children. We loved each other, but we got... stuck. I needed the pack, and she agreed to move back here, but she never fully understood why."

I need to change the subject before I delve too much into nostalgia. "Did you always know you were a demon?"

Vicky shifts in my arms. "No. I'm an orphan, and I was raised in a human family. We aren't born craving sex. We are awakened to our true nature after puberty by drinking demon blood."

"Wow. If you'd never drunk..."

"I'd still be human, yes. But I was giving off pheromones or something, because demons found me pretty quickly." There's a cringe hidden in there, behind her meek tone and her light smile. "It was confusing at first, but thankfully, I didn't think sex was a sin."

How many times has she fed on someone she didn't like? How many men forced themselves on her? I can't imagine what her life has been like, really, and wonder if she ever put down roots.

I search her face for an answer. "Would Dominic's health be in jeopardy if you only fed on him?"

"Of course not."

"So, you don't *need* multiple partners?"

Her muscles tense, her nose wrinkling.

"I'm not saying you shouldn't—" My cheeks heat up. "It was a doctor's question, sorry." I brush my thumb against the nape of her neck. "Lust, sex, repeat... It sounds lonely."

"It's awesome." Her grin doesn't quite warm her eyes.

"Do you ever stay in one place long enough for more?" I have to know. It's selfish as hell, but I have to know if I'll wake up one morning to find her gone.

The shrug she serves me is anything but casual, her shoulders stiff, and her dismissive wave shaky. "The world awaits."

Something in my gut tells me it's not her choice, and I press my forehead to hers, testing a theory I've been nurturing for some time now. "What are you running from? What's your last name, Vicky?" DeLuca struck a nerve the other night, and I need to know why. How can an apparently innocuous question incite such a fearful response in a girl that's otherwise fearless?

She struggles to break free from my embrace. "I can't—"

"Shh. It's okay. We don't have to talk about it."

But she's still trembling, her teeth chattering, her heart racing. It's the tell-tale signs of deep psychological trauma, and my fists clench. Whoever hurt her should suffer eternal punishment.

I draw slow circles across her back until her breathing returns to normal, and the stench of fear recedes. "It's your turn. Ask me another question."

She traces the collar of my shirt. "Gabriel told me you got wounded in the war?"

"Yes. August 1945."

"No wonder you're so old-fashioned."

I rest my chin against her neck. "I don't think you can call me old-fashioned after what happened yesterday..."

"You feel guilty."

"Yes. I shouldn't have watched without your permission. And Dom's. It wasn't a mistake, I knew full well what you were doing, and I completely disregarded your privacy. I was curious and hard. No mitigating circumstances."

With a brisk shake of the head, she cups my cheeks, smiling like I'm silly. "We both thought it was hot as hell."

"Still..."

"Hey. Sex isn't some evil thing. You said it yourself. It's a basic human need. Sex, food, shelter. You have to recognize that your guilt doesn't come from a good place. It's a way of thinking some old monks imposed to lay their claim on women and force them to stay chaste before marriage, reinforcing a patriarchy that lasted for millenniums. It's not like being kind vs cruel or killing vs helping. Sexuality is good."

"I'm a doctor, remember. There are medical drawbacks to sex, not just moral ones."

She tugs on my collar. "Not for us. We can't catch STDs, and there's zero risk of an unplanned pregnancy."

"You can't get pregnant?" I watch her face closely.

She doesn't break eye contact. "I'm a half-breed demon. We can't have kids."

"It doesn't bother you?"

"No. I'm perfectly okay not having kids. If I wanted to, I could adopt." There's nothing in her voice that rings untrue or forced. She's perfectly okay with it, and again I feel the weight of my real age. Most women I diagnosed with infertility were crushed, but Vicky is different. And the times have changed.

"I get to live sickness-free for centuries. It's not a bad lot," she says.

My mind screeches to a halt, my heart suddenly pumping so fast that the rush of blood to my head is dizzying. "You do not age as a human?"

"Nope."

I crush my mouth to hers, and she squeals in delight. Her soft lips are heaven, her tongue expertly blurring my inhibitions and igniting a fiery path from my mouth to my chest and down to my already painful erection. If there was ever an argument in favor of opening my heart again, the knowledge that I won't have to go through the wretched reality of watching the woman I love die of old age is a big one.

I nip her earlobe. Her back arches, and her hand travels south, her nails raking against my crotch.

My eyes flutter, but I grip her wrist and return her hand to the front, hugging her tight. "Not yet."

"Why not?" She twists in my grasp. "You want me. Why wait?"

"Why rush?"

Her breathing hitches, and she hugs her chest. "I need to feed."

Just as I thought. "Dominic will be home soon."

"You'd rather hand me off to him *again* than experience it for yourself?" Her tone is teasing, not annoyed.

I rub a smudge of red lipstick off her chin. "When we have sex, it's going to be epic. And it's going to mean something."

A melodic moan rises from her chest. "I like epic."

Dom barrels down the driveway in his truck, and the headlights roar across the dark living room.

When he enters the house, she struts to him, links her arms around his neck, and crushes her mouth to his.

It shouldn't bother me to see them kiss. Dom staked his claim first, and I'm the third wheel. The only reason I'm in the mix at all is because of her nature and his kinky spirit. Still... I can't seem to tear my gaze away from them. Dom grips her waist, his hands slipping under her shirt, and I wonder what it would have felt like to surrender.

A pang of regret squeezes my stomach as Dom picks her up and walks off to his room, her legs tight around his waist.

And I almost follow.

SEXY BOY

VICKY

"Thank you again," Billie says, her tanned legs dangling from the back of Gabriel's black pick-up truck.

The hood of a second, almost identical truck is propped open in front of her. Gabriel is lying underneath, his shoulders and head hidden by the bumper.

I take my pulse, my muscles tingling all over from my grueling run in the woods, and watch the driveway from the end of the trail. The wind is non-existent, so I know they haven't smelled me yet. Tall trees shield this side of the house from the sun, but the driveway is unprotected.

Billie tucks a long strand of brown hair behind her ear. "Jeff couldn't find what was wrong with it."

"Jeff is losing his touch." The alpha slides from underneath the bumper. Black oil and dust are smeared across his gray t-shirt. He stretches the bottom and wipes his forehead with it, revealing a string of tattoos and a perfect six-pack.

I hold my breath as he stands and strips from the cotton, using the whole thing to pat down his face. A sheen of sweat glistens over his body.

He doesn't look dirty. He looks fuck hot.

He tilts his head back and gulps down his water bottle. Billie's breasts strain against her top, her chest heaving. Her sight is riveted on the alpha's robust body. I prance over to them, interrupting their little *tête-à-tête*.

"Car trouble?" I ask.

"Hm, yeah," Billie answers, her eyes darting to me but quickly returning to Gabriel.

The young brunette's attire—denim shorts that barely cover her ass and a white wife beater—leave nothing to the imagination. Her black bra is visible underneath, and I wiggle my brows at Gabriel behind Billie's back.

We have a silent conversation.

I arch a brow. *Fake car troubles?*

He scowls. *Yeah, so what?*

I bite back a chuckle. "I get the appeal, but it's too big."

Billie's shoulders tense. "Mm?"

I run my fingers over the curves of her car. "Pick-up trucks. They're so big, and they use too much gas. Haven't you heard? There's an energy crisis coming."

On his way to the open garage, Gabriel's eyes lock with mine, and he chucks out a gruff *woof*. My gaze slips down his back, entranced by how his dark blue jeans hug his ass, and I wet my lips.

I can practically feel the poor girl behind me trying to control her breathing. Being mischievous, I send a bit of lust her way, and the scent of her arousal quickly fills the air.

She shuffles to her feet, blushing deep red. "I—I should go. My shift is coming up."

"It should start fine now," Gabriel returns to her hood, slams it shut, and wipes his oiled hands down with a rag.

I don't think either of them noticed my discrete interference and grin.

"Thank you." Billie hops in her truck, wrenches it in gear, and backs out of the driveway.

As she turns the corner, I lean towards the alpha. "Now, why don't you put that girl out of her misery?"

"Who I fuck and when is none of your business. Stop messing with her." Taking another swig of water, a moan of approval passes his lips and totally derails my concentration. He swipes the back of his big, masculine hand across his mouth.

Damn that wolf is hot.

I raise my palms in surrender. "Just saying." A cheeky smile glazes my lips. "Or maybe you prefer blondes?"

Gabriel crushes the plastic bottle in his hands, a million tiny crackles making me shiver, before he tosses it into the trash. He meets my stare with a dark chuckle and an even darker frown. "I'm partial to redheads."

My stomach cramps. *So are all my exes.*

I follow him inside. Sam is typing on his laptop at the island, his slender fingers flying across the keys, and I skip over to him, wrapping my arms around his neck from behind.

Gabriel grabs a new water bottle from the fridge and twists the cap open.

"That's also bad for the environment," I say, leaning against Sam.

Gabriel flips me off with a smile.

Dom bursts into the kitchen, the porch door swinging on its hinges. His brows are furrowed, his boyish face twisted up with worry. "Tell me again why you didn't tell us about your plan?"

Gabe sips on his water. "What's up with you?"

Dom snatches the bottle from him. "I was running, thinking over your plan, and it doesn't make sense."

"I needed you to keep an eye on Evelyn," Gabriel says, his eyes narrowed like he's about to murder Dom for stealing his water away.

"Doesn't explain why you didn't tell us. You could have died..." Dom's voice breaks, and he paces the living room and back.

I shoot Gabriel an accusing glare.

The gruff alpha clears his throat. "I didn't tell you because there's a mole in the pack."

Dom and Sam barely pick up their jaws off the floor in time to say, "What?"

"Xavier knew about my trip to the last detail, and someone had to tip him off that I'd found the weapon depot," Gabriel announces.

Sam pushes his laptop aside, and I can see the cogs of his brain turning.

Dom throws his arms in the air. "Why didn't you tell us sooner? I could have figured out who it was. I could have—" He comes to an abrupt stop. His knuckles clench around the back of a chair. "You thought it might be one of us..." His jaw ticks. "You thought it might be *me*." Betrayal and disappointment render his usually upbeat voice totally unrecognizable.

Something passes between Gabe and I.

"Of course not. I thought it might be *her*, and I knew you couldn't keep a secret," he says.

I nod in understanding at the lie. Gabriel fucked up by not trusting Dominic, but he won't make that mistake again. I can play his game to spare Dom's feelings.

The young wolf exhales loudly. "Stupid alpha."

Gabriel's pupils are all black. "What did you say?"

"Nothing, boss." Dom pauses. "Just don't... I'm—*We're* all on *your* side. You know that, right?" He tilts his head, a boyish expression softening his face.

Dom isn't as naïve as they pegged him to be, and I hide a proud grin behind my hand.

Gabe swallows hard. "I do."

"'Cause you two..." Dom looks to Sam. "You're my family."

Suddenly, I feel like I'm intruding and scratch at a knot in the cherry-wood table.

Gabriel squeezes Dom's shoulder. "I know, kid. I know. I just—I'm a paranoid old fuck."

A big smile breaks on my boyfriend's face. "Yeah, you are." He snags an apple from the fruit basket and bites down on it. "We'll get the bastard. Don't worry, I'll figure it out, boss."

The heavy atmosphere recedes.

Dom clasps my hand. "There's a party at the springs tonight to celebrate our victory, you wanna go?"

"Sounds fun." I turn to Sam. His eyes are still wide with shock. "You should come with us."

"Err—" the doctor chokes on his answer.

I twine our fingers. "Pleeeease."

He nods.

Holding hands with both my handsome, smart, incredible wolves, I beam and turn to Gabriel. "And you?"

The alpha walks toward his room.

"Does it ever get lonely down there?" I yell after him.

He waves with his back to us and disappears down the staircase. "There's not a soul alive who's been down there besides me, and I love it that way."

AVALANCHE

VICKY

Since I can't turn into a wolf and run to the party, Sam drives to the closest parking spot, and we hike the rest of the way on foot.

"You're too slow." Dominic throws me over his shoulder, and I giggle.

Music booms louder and louder through the pines as we draw close. The sun hasn't set yet, but a big fire is already raging in the large clearing. A copious expanse of rocks is flanked by blue waters, and the contrast between the lush, green vegetation is beautiful. To top it off, a waterfall spills into the lake.

There's at least thirty people drinking and chatting, some of them skinny-dipping, others dancing by the fire. Piles of clothes lay everywhere, and a few furry wolves come and go.

"They look young," I remark.

Dominic waves to a few guys sitting by the huge speakers. "I look twenty, yet I'm thirty." He walks to them, and I stay behind with Sam.

"The youngest here is Lena, don't worry. And I'm by far the oldest." His shoulders wiggle, and he eyes the crowd with a fearful frown.

I press my palm to his chest. "Let me guess. You don't usually come to these parties?"

"No."

Dom hands us each a beer and raises his own. "To Sam's first night out in forever."

"To Sam," I say with a bright smile.

We all chug a few mouthfuls down, but beer is not an efficient way to get me drunk.

My gaze darts around the flocks of young wolves, and I meet Lena's stare. She's sitting by the lake, her black and blue hair wet and sticking to her neck. A white, translucent shirt clings to her skin. A few boys are staring directly at her chest, but she doesn't seem to mind or notice. She waves me over and elbows a girl I've never seen before, pointing in my direction.

I dash over to them.

Lena's voice is high with excitement. The beer in her hands is clearly not her first. "Vicky. This is my best friend, Jenny."

"Hey," I greet her friend, getting a small smile in return.

"Jen wanted to ask you—" Lena starts.

"Shut up, Lena," Jenny whines, turning all shades of red.

I try to keep a straight face. "What did you want to ask me?"

Both girls nod to the side, and we walk closer to the falls.

Lena lowers her voice, but her drunken whispers are still too loud. "Jen wants to lose her *virginity* tonight. Obviously, I'm the also-a-virgin, useless confidante, so—"

Jenny's eyes are wide, and she elbows her friend hard in the stomach.

Swallowing back a smile, I sit atop a big rock. "Ask away."

"I told you." Lena proudly pulls her drink to her lips.

"Does it hurt?" Jenny asks.

"It might sting a little, but if you kiss and touch each other for a while first, it will hurt less. It should feel great for you, too. Don't let him get lazy. If you have an orgasm before he gets naked, that's even better."

"It's just—I felt *it* the other day, and it's *big*."

Lena almost chokes on her bottle's rim. "Ew. TMI." She stalks off, leaving Jenny and I alone.

A cute boy is stealing glances at us.

I scratch my arm and point to him discreetly. "Is that him?"

Jenny blushes. "Yes. We've been together for a few months, and I love him. I want to, but I don't know what to do."

"You'll figure it out. Just don't do anything you don't want to do and tell him what feels good and what doesn't—" I dangle my legs from the edge of the rock. "But you know, boys are sometimes stressed out, too, so emphasize the good. Size shouldn't make it hurt more if you're enjoying yourself." I wink. "It might even make it better."

Her lips quirk up. "Lena was right about you. You're cool."

She returns to her boyfriend, and I watch my guys from a distance. They're chatting animatedly.

Sam takes a sip of beer, and I've seen him drink wine at dinner before, but I can't stop staring. With the black cotton shirt hugging his chest and the fire dancing on his face, he's so different. The wind plays with his hair, leaving his short curls all in disarray.

Dom's lips move quickly as he and Sam go back and forth, deep in conversation.

Their words are swallowed by the rumble of the falls and the music, but Sam laughs, his chiseled features stretching into a stunning smile. Desire rumbles in my belly.

Unable to stop myself, I hurry back to them and crush my mouth to Sam's.

His hand clamps around my shoulder like he's going to push me away, but he pulls me to him instead. His thumb brushes against the back of my ear, and I hook my arms around his neck. Beer and fun on his breath, he's the best kisser I ever met.

My skin tingles deliciously as I emerge.

The others are all staring at us, either with wide eyes, arms crossed, or knowing smirks.

I raise my beer to the crowd. "I'm dating two guys. Anyone here have a problem with that?"

One tall boy uses his hands to shout, "No, Ma'am."

They all laugh and return to their conversations. The youth in this town is more worldly than I expected. Just enough MTV got through, I guess.

Sam snakes an arm around my waist, keeping me in his lap, and Dom reclines against the stone at his back, totally comfortable.

They introduce me to a bunch of people, and with all the new faces, I'm pretty sure I won't remember all those names. A few sit with us and chat. They tell me funny stories about Dom or gossip about the other wolves. It's not like hanging out with humans, either. They do not stare as much, and I no longer feel like the sex-kitten/pariah *du jour*.

The moon is high in the sky, the fire smoldering, when Lena comes up to us. "We're all going for a run. Sorry, Vicky, wolf-costume mandatory."

Dom waves her off. "Go. We're fine here."

"I see that," she snickers.

They filter out one by one until we're alone, abandoned clothes peppering the rocks. Shifters have many sins, but modesty isn't one of them.

Something passes between my wolves, and the atmosphere thickens. Then, like they planned the choreography perfectly, Dom crawls over to me and encircles my shoulders while Sam deposits my ass on the ground. They lay me down, and Dom holds both my hands above my head, touching only my wrists.

With nothing but a thick blanket and stone at my back, I draw in a sharp breath. "What's this?"

"An experiment," Sam answers with a devilish grin.

The slight slope makes it easy for him to reach up and drag my pants down my body. His nails scrape along my thighs, and he wrangles the jeans past the kink of my knees to finish peeling them off. He pauses over my tattoo, his fingers tracing the shape of the ink splatter, but he doesn't mention it.

Dom wrestles with my shirt, passing it over my head and out one arm at a time. The promise dancing in his eyes softens my knees. I can't quite believe what's happening, to be honest.

I search Sam's dark blue eyes for an answer. "What happened to your stance on sex and feelings?"

"I owe you one," he leans in and whispers the rest in my ear, "And I've got plenty of *feelings*." Sam pulls his own shirt off, his abs rippling under my heated stare. He pushes my thighs apart, making space for himself, and runs a hand from the space between my breasts to my navel before traveling back up. Each migration creeps closer to my breasts and lower down my belly, and I squirm.

Dom's hands snake behind my back to unhook my bra, and Sam flings it to the side. The cool night air blows over my sensitive skin.

My nipples harden.

This is really fucking happening.

Sam's throat bobs. He looks down at me like I'm a juicy orange ripe for the picking. He palms my left breast, then my right, testing their weight. A low grunt rumbles at the back of his throat. "Hold her tight." The richness of his voice smolders deep inside my core.

Sam unleashes the full power of his talented mouth on my breasts, his tongue swirling around the taut peaks while his hands caress the inside of my thighs. When he starts heading lower down my belly, I pant, "Please."

"Patience, baby," Dom whispers into my ear.

Hot fingers massage my inner thigh, pulling back on the brink of my soaked entrance only to return and tease me some more.

I groan when Sam finally slides a finger inside me, but I'm so wet and wanting I can barely feel it.

The doctor's intense gaze never breaks contact as he starts caressing me from the inside, his brows bent in concentration. He studies my every reactions like he wants to write a thesis on the depths of my pleasure.

When he bends down and sucks on my clit, my eyes roll inward. "God, yes. More." Sam destroys me with his mouth, my legs parting even wider, and my climax is already banging at the door.

"Fuck. It's hot as hell." Dom's tongue slips between my lips, rough and demanding.

This is new to me, and I come from the sheer singularity of the moment. For all the sex I've had and the talk I talk, I haven't had the best of luck with threesomes. Two men certainly never pinned me down to pleasure *me*.

Dom chuckles at how quick it was, but Sam doesn't stop, gripping my quivering legs, bringing me to yet another edge. His tongue starts tracing wider and wider circles, shying away from where I need him most. I wiggle, trying to break free, but they deny me. They have sole control. It drives me nuts.

"This is torture," I cry out.

He keeps going father and farther, the rhythm unchanged, but the distance making me shake with need. I struggle against Dom, but he laughs and holds me in place, his mouth fastening around my nipple.

"God. I'll get revenge for this, I swear."

Sam stops, and his eyes flash with hunger. He blows over my clit, the pressure of his breath against my hot, greedy core making me mad. His tongue flicks the sensitive bud exactly once, and the second orgasm shatters me, unfurling again and again while he watches, my walls clenching forcefully around emptiness.

I curse and bless his name.

The bulge in his pants must be painful by now, but he doesn't move.

Dom releases my arms, and I lunge at Sam, but he clamps my wrists and pulls them to his shoulders. The warm planes of his chest feel amazing against my bare chest.

"You're sure you don't want..." Dom asks from behind me, the sound of his zipper making me quake in anticipation.

Sam cups my face, his thumbs caressing my jawline. "Soon."

Dom's smooth head drags against my ass, the tip wet. Sam kisses me exactly as Dom enters me, and I meet the slam of his hips with a wildness that surprises even me. My breasts drag against Sam's torso with each thrust. I want Sam inside me. Hell, I want them both inside me. Preferably at the same time.

"How does she feel?" Sam asks, peeking over my shoulder and stealing all my thoughts.

Dom's voice is hoarse. "Fucking perfect. Tight. Wet. She has muscles down there I've never felt before. You won't last a minute the first time."

Hearing them chat is impossibly erotic, and I shudder when Dom hits a particularly delicious spot.

Sam tends to my breasts, rolling them in his strong hands, pushing them together and releasing them only to see them bounce before he starts all over again. I know he's imagining what it would fell like to fuck them.

Dom's cock gets even deeper, and I cry out.

He rides me hard and fast like he wants to rip me in two. "Let go, baby."

I come with Sam's tongue in my mouth, his hands on my breasts, the sensations more potent than anything I've ever felt. And I realize... I'm not feeding right now. I'm just having sex.

And it's incredible.

BILLY S

VICKY

The little bell above the green door of the hair salon jiggles as I walk in. About five heads, some with rollers, others with aluminum foil, glare at me. From the way they turn up their noses, you'd think those salon chairs are thrones, and that I've just walked into the Queen of England's secret Oregonian beauty parlor.

But the sign in the window clearly said *Selene's Fur-tastic Styles.*

"What are you doing here?" a curvy blond woman asks. Her skin is smooth, but the out-of-control volume of her skewed ponytail screams 80's fashion victim. She's the only one wearing an apron, so I figure she's Selene.

I'm not fond of the way she's pointing those sharp scissors at my face.

The door closes behind me with a bang, and I tap the floor with my red heels.

A few royal citizens of Wolf Creek steal glances at my legs.

"It's a hair salon, isn't it? I'm here for a haircut." My tone is slightly more defensive than what I was aiming for. I thought that—on the account of me being a total hero for saving Gabriel—the older female population would have warmed up to me a little.

But she-wolves will be she-wolves.

The hairdresser's scissors finally return to her customer's bangs. "Go back to where you came from."

I cock my hip to the side. "And where is that?"

"You're a demon, no? Whatever hell you crawled out from."

A lanky teenage boy glowers from the sinks, his white-foam covered hands rising in the air. "Mom! Will you stop? She helped us kill Xavier."

Selene's scissors draw quick patterns in the empty space between her and the boy. "Mind your own business, Niko."

"It's okay. I'll leave. I wouldn't want you near my hair anyway." My knuckles are white against the door handle, the bell already chiming above me.

I stomp down the dirty road and fumble with the buttons on my phone. Gabriel gave it back to me now that I'm no longer on his suspect list. He even programmed in his number. I walked here from City Hall, leaving Dominic to his super-secret mission.

Sam and Gabe have been AWOL for almost 30 hours. Last night was the full moon, and I know they took in a bunch of Xavier's wolves. Gabriel absolutely forbade me from visiting the newbies before he made sure that they were all upstanding citizens.

I really wanted a haircut. My hair grows faster than humans and creeps toward my butt. I guess I'll buy a pair of scissors at the general store and give myself a serious trim.

Lena's blue Toyota pulls up next to me, the huge Snoopy bumper sticker making me grin.

She rolls down her window, and the wind plays with her knotty dark locks. "Hey."

"How did you know I was here?"

"I was right across the street when Niko texted that his Mom was a total bitch to you."

I lean against her car. "So you decided to come to my rescue?"

"In a way. Selene is so old-fashioned that there was a need for a... trendier hairdresser. I've been cutting people's hair since I was fourteen."

"Why didn't you say so!" I walk around the bumper and yank open the passenger door, plopping down on the seat next to her.

Lena presses on the accelerator, laughing, and drives into yet another woodsy dead-end. I'm seeing a pattern emerge in wolf real estate.

Her house is a lot like ours but older, the triangle roof thick with vines, and the large wrap-around porch needs a fresh coat of white paint.

She kicks her shoes off over the doormat, and I do the same before she pulls me inside.

"Hey, Dad. This is Vicky. Vicky, this is my dad, Jeff Dawson," she says.

The man sitting at the kitchen table folds his newspaper. "I know who she is." He's got bright hazel eyes and a proud chin. A tiny hint of gray is visible at his blond temples, but he doesn't look a day over forty. He clears his throat and glowers in my direction. "You shouldn't be here."

Lena huffs. "She needs a haircut, and Selene wouldn't touch her. So... deal with it."

Deep lines appear on his forehead. "Okay then, but the door stays open."

"Don't worry, Mr. Dawson. I'm not here to seduce your daughter," I say with a respectful, non-threatening smile.

The poor man almost chokes on his coffee, and Lena snorts. She links her arm in mine and leads me away.

The layout of the first floor is also a lot like ours, with the open kitchen and living room out front and the bedrooms in the back, but Lena's room is smaller.

She wasn't kidding about being the town's back-up hairdresser. A big chair is sitting in front a huge wall mirror, various products displayed on the wicker table. Piles of make-up and nail polish burst out of matching baskets. "You do nails?"

"Of course."

I notice the pink-and-black stripes embellishing her hands. "Nice." My previously manicured nails are in dire need of a refresh.

Lena's room is chaotic to say the least, but the blue, black and pink accents totally match her personality. The posters on the walls make me grin. "Crushing on Hailee Steinfeld, are you?"

She nods emphatically. "Totally."

The picture of a blond woman is set next to her queen-sized bed, and I run my fingers along the frame. "Is that your mother? She's a beauty."

"Was. She died seven years ago. It was a stupid accident at the colony. Xavier and Gabriel were friends back then, and Mom wanted to try the living-closer-to-humans thing. She did it for me, so I could have a less reclusive life. But a volatile wolf shifted in the middle of the suburbs. My mother tried to save him. She got shot, and by the time Sam got to her, it was too late." Tears glass over her piercing green eyes.

A ball forms in my throat. "I'm sorry."

"Me too." She wipes her cheek discreetly.

"Do you have any brothers or sisters?" The house is small, but wolves live for so long, she might have older siblings.

She motions for me to sit in the salon chair. "No. Shifter DNA is messed-up, it's not rare for couples to have only one child. It took my parents nearly four decades to have me, but it might have been because of the blood thing."

"What blood thing?"

She wraps a black vinyl coverall around my neck. "Remember my appointment the other day? When you asked why I came to see Sam? I—I'm sick." She avoids my gaze in the mirror, her eyes fixed on my hair. She wets it with a water spray, droplets misting my face.

My brows furrow. "Sick? I thought you guys didn't get sick."

"It's some rare wolf shifter disease. It started about a year and a half ago. I need these blood markers that I can't make myself to fend off this weird auto-immune crap, so Sam transfuses me every month or so."

I swallow hard. "Are you going to be okay?"

"I should be." She passes her fingers through my hair. "I'm so jealous. Mine is always knotty and dry. Yours look good when you get out of bed, I'm sure." She clearly doesn't want to dwell on her sickness.

"It's because of what I am. Even my hair is made to attract," I explain.

"That's nice."

The silence is heavy.

"Cut it to my shoulders. I need a change," I say, trying to break the tension.

Her jaw slacks. "To your shoulders? Are you sure?" She pulls my mane in a fist and grabs her scissors. "Last chance to change your mind."

"Cut away. It grows like weed."

"Now, I'm really jealous." She sticks out her tongue.

A loud snipping sound follows, and I feel ten pounds lighter already.

An opened letter on her desk catches my attention. It's from Yale University. I graze the envelope. "You're going to college?"

She swiftly grabs the letter and dumps it in her dresser. "Maybe."

"Why only maybe?"

"My friends are all going to UC Davis next year. I'm not sure if I can wait." The steady pace of the scissors is interrupted by a few nervous tugs.

"You could bring a human boyfriend back for Christmas. I'm sure your father and Gabriel would love that," I joke.

She cracks a smile. "Unless I want to spend the rest of my life in exile, I should visit my imaginary boyfriend's family instead."

Is she saying she can't bring a human home? "But Sam's wife moved here after he was bitten?"

"Disclosing our existence to humans isn't allowed anymore. With all the technology, it's too dangerous to expose ourselves."

Makes sense, I guess. Every species has stricter rules now that phones can record and photograph every little supernatural thing. On the other hand, the advancements in photoshop and image manipulation have also helped. People aren't willing to believe everything they see anymore, and that works in our favor.

Lena separates my hair in the middle and evens out the cut. "Thanks for helping Jen the other day. She was really stressed out. She told me to tell you that he didn't get lazy at all." Lena blushes deep red at that.

"Don't you have sex ed or something?"

"The teachers at the school have been there since the early 60s. The best they managed during sex ed was to show us pictures of litters of puppies to freak us out."

I choke on my breath. Lena looks dead serious.

The uncontrollable giggles that follow attract her father's attention.

"What's going on here?" Mr. Dawson asks.

The laughter doubles, and Lena and I are fighting for breath.

"Nothing," she manages to chuck out in between snorts.

Her father hovers in the doorway like he's looking for a reason to stick around and watch over us. "So, did Gabriel mention what he planned to do with Evelyn?"

"Nope." I guess I understand his point of view. If my teenage daughter had an incubus friend, I'd be watching that dude like a hawk.

Jeff shifts his weight from one foot to the other. "I thought he'd ask me to track her, that's all."

"I think he asked Dominic," I say with a reassuring smile.

Lena shakes her head rapidly and opens her palm to the ceiling. "Dad. You're being nosy. Get out!"

The man grumbles but obeys.

I chuckle. "He looks nice."

"He's a great dad but a total nuisance. He asks me all these questions *all* the time. And I'm like... Dad! You don't need to know every word I exchanged with everyone I crossed paths with. Be normal." Lena's sweet laugh tells me that she knows how lucky she is.

SHAKE IT OUT

VICKY

*L*ena drops me off at the cabin. I sit on the porch, soaking in the rainy summer day. Fall is coming; I better enjoy the heat while I can. The clouds press the draft-less, humid day on my shoulders, but I welcome the heat. The easy-going, relaxed vibe of this rural life suits me more than I expected. I'm more rock-and-roll than country, but maybe this is a chance to reconsider a lot of thing I thought I knew about myself.

Sam emerges from the woods. Pine cones crunch under his feet and sweat sticks to his neck. A big leather bag is braced over his shoulder, a serious look stuck on his face. His curls are sticking out in different directions, and his button-down blue shirt is all crumpled.

The lines on his face ease up when he sees me, and I skip closer to him. He slows his strides so we're shoulder to shoulder.

"Hey. Haven't seen you in more than a day. Where are you going?" I ask.

He points to the large shed behind the garage but remains silent on his whereabouts.

"I went into town this morning and then Lena's for a haircut." I pout, a bit cross that he hasn't commented on my new look and doesn't appear at all interested in doing so. But I've got bigger worries. "Lena told me... she explained her blood disease. Is she really going to be okay?"

The question jolts him out of his silence. "Yes. I found a cure."

"But she'll need transfusions for the rest of her life?"

"Probably." He's still not meeting my gaze, and his voice rings higher than it should. He's hiding something.

I step in front of him, blocking his path. Metal clanks from the bag as he dumps it to the ground and pulls me in for a kiss. While his expression said *fed up with the world* barely two seconds ago, his tongue is deep into *missed you terribly* territory. I hum against his mouth, his stubble scratching my face. I've never seen him less than freshly shaved and run my fingers against his cheek. "I'm digging the rough look."

He rests his forehead against mine and skims my hair with his hands. "You look amazing. Lena's an artist."

"What's up with the bag?" Leaning down, I tug on the zipper, curious, and push aside the flap. A frown settles on my face at the big metal cuffs linked to meters and meters of chains. "Secretly filming a BDSM movie in the woods?"

He cracks up. "I wish."

I smack his shoulder. "Spill the beans, doctor. Where were you?"

"I helped Gabriel steady the new recruits through the full moon. It was... violent." Shadows dance on his face, the weight of his restless night clearly taking a toll of him.

There's dried blood on his neck.

I hook my arms around his elbow and pull him along. "Come on. Let's get you in the shower."

He follows me like a puppy on a leash to the bathroom.

With a sigh, I close the door behind him, eyes screwed shut. The water turns on. I consider joining him, but he's not in the right state of mind.

My body hums at the crisp, mental image of water dripping down Sam's body. Truth is, since the party, I haven't been able to think about anything else other than the hunger brimming in his eyes when I came around his fingers. And against his mouth.

I rub my arms to chase the chill, but my mind has short-circuited. It's singing a *Get Sam Naked* song, and there's no switching the channel.

Trying to distract myself from the filthy scenarios clawing my brain, I go back outside.

Dom has new scratches on his face and a discrete limp. He's hosing the chains down, the water and metal reflecting the light of the setting sun.

I lean against the house. "What happened to you two?"

"The last 24 hours were... savage. It was rough on Sam." The gold and hazel flecks in his eyes gleam. "Love the hair."

I push myself off the wall and walk to him. "Are you guys heading back out?"

His arms snake around me, molding me to him. "Gabriel and I are going to check on them, but the full moon is over." His lips find mine, but his kiss is gentle instead of hungry. "Keep Sam here and make him feel better, will you?" Dom winks.

He's leaving us alone by design.

My lips twitch, and I consider the chains at my feet with mischief. I've got just the idea.

HALF AN HOUR after Dom's departure, Sam finally exits the bathroom. He's squeaky clean, wearing only jeans, his bare chest on display.

I notice he didn't shave. "Come here." I plant a voluptuous kiss on him, testing the waters.

He groans against my mouth, his hands flying to my neck.

"Do you want to sleep or eat or—" I start.

He kisses me again, his breath heavy.

"Close your eyes." With a smile, I clasp his hand and guide him deep inside his room. "Hold your arms up."

His brows furrow. "Why?"

"Trust me." I stand on my tiptoes and hook the cuff hanging from the wood beam above us around his right wrist.

His eyes snap open. "What—"

"This is my revenge." I shackle his other hand.

His Adam's apple bobs, his arms now tied above his head. He glances up for a short second.

I follow his worried gaze. "Is the beam strong enough to hold you?"

"The roof sits on it," he says in lieu of a *yes*.

"Try not to pull down the roof, then."

A nervous chuckle pops out of his damn sexy mouth. "Why do I need to be chained to the ceiling?"

"Because that way you have to relinquish control. And it'll give you fonder memories of the chains as a bonus," I say, pecking his lips.

The incredulity and hesitation painted on his face melt, his darkening gaze slipping down my cleavage.

He's no puritan—the other day speaks for itself—but he's still tense.

I kiss him until he relaxes and pull my shirt off. I'm wearing my black, plunging bra and matching underwear, and Sam looks mesmerized by the sight. I claim his mouth again, and we sink into the kiss. His skin feels so warm, so right beneath my fingers. I trace the ridge of his abs down to his Adonis belt and dip my head down to flick his nipple with my tongue.

The button of his jeans is easy to pop, and I spread his zipper open.

Sam groans. He's warm and heavy in my hand when I palm him over his boxers. Dom never wears them, the hassle of underwear too much to bother with considering he needs to strip before changing into a wolf, but Sam's more traditional.

Unable to pace myself, I peel the cotton back.

A sharp inhale rocks his breath as I touch his bare flesh for the first time. I kneel in front of him and meet his gaze.

He nods almost imperceptibly, telling me he's okay with this.

He's a sight to behold. The shy doctor bites down on his bottom lip, his big, beautiful cock jutting out of his too-clean jeans. I run my tongue from the base to the tip, and his feet leave the ground for a second. He tastes like soap and salted caramel. Delicious. Forbidden.

This is not just another hookup. He hasn't been with a woman in a while, and I want to be worthy of the transgression.

A desperate clench between my legs makes me groan. Desire tightens my abdominal muscles, my arousal dripping along my thighs. God. I don't think I've ever been so turned on. The anticipation from the last couple of weeks makes it all sweeter somehow. It takes all my self-control not to scrap my original plan and set Sam free so I can sink upon his gloriously long and thick length. Instead, I wrap my lips around his head and take him as deep as I can.

He cries out.

I feast on his hooded eyes, his balled fists, and the poorly concealed moans.

I can see how badly he's trying not to thrust inside my mouth, not to do anything un-Sam. It drives me crazy with lust, the incomparable need to wake his beast blazing in my belly. I scrape the tip with my teeth, wrap my hand around the base, and squeeze.

"Ah, Vicky."

I tease the crown again, giving a good lick to the underside, and Sam curses.

His blue eyes are dark, and his hips grind against my mouth. He's always so controlled, but not now.

Never before have I wished more for a rough hand at the back of my neck telling me I'm doing it right.

"Stop, please."

I snicker and take him deeper.

"I'm serious, Vicky. I want to come inside you," he croaks.

Okay. Now we're talking.

The second I get rid of the cuffs, his hands are on me, touching my face, my breasts, my waist, my ass. I yank down his pants, and we both freeze.

White and red lines swirl into a blotch of scars over his right knee like it was blown off and barely pieced back together. My fingers tremble over the flesh. "Oh, Sam."

Our heavy breaths collide as he pulls me to him. He kisses me stupid, one slow kiss after another, his tongue ravishing my mouth with ferocious tenderness, It's a dizzying mix of care and animal need that only Sam can blend so seamlessly. I revel in the affection radiating off him, his eyes roving over me like I'm more than a beautiful face. More than a woman he wants to fuck. More than life.

He hooks an arm below my knees, carrying me to the bed. My bra and underwear are cast aside, replaced by his mouth and hands.

One, two, then three fingers brush my center. He preps me for his girth, but I'm so ready, I'm shaking.

Our gazes connect when he aligns himself with my slick tightness.

His nose traces a path from my collarbone to my ear. "I know you'll think I'm crazy. That it's too fast. I have to say it anyway. I love you, Vicky."

I hold my breath. I haven't heard these words in years. Not in earnest.

Men never say these words when they feel a woman isn't prepared to say them back, and I certainly can't say them myself.

Once, I said them to the wrong man, and it almost cost me my soul.

But Sam isn't anything like him. Sam is gentle and generous. He could never hurt a woman on purpose, and he has wormed himself into my heart.

I stand on the brink, his calm gaze telling me he'll accept my silence. He doesn't need to hear it back.

He can wait.

My mouth is dry, so I steal a kiss.

"I—" My voice cracks, and I shake in his arms. The words are there, almost formed, ringing so clearly in my mind that they reach a dusty, abandoned nook inside my heart.

The secrets and lies between us hold them back. He loves Vicky, but that's not really my name. In this instant, I wish it was. I wish I could rewrite my past and change the end of my story to a *happy ever after*. I wish it *so much*.

The patient wolf worships my body, fucking me slow and steady. It's heady and new. I'm floating on Sam's cloud, his arms carrying me to a whole other place. He whispers words of love in my ears, his touch painting me like a canvas, the strokes creating rainbows of pleasure across my skin. Our bodies crash together like poetry, our gasps rhyming, the verses full of kisses.

His blue eyes pull me deeper and deeper into that incredible connection, and I come and come around his thick shaft, crushing him to me, moaning his name.

He throbs to completion inside me, our climaxes as aligned as our hearts in this perfect love bubble.

"Oh God, Vicky. That was..." he seals the sentence with a kiss.

I'm still catching my breath. He holds me to him and nuzzles my neck, our fingers twined over my stomach. The intimacy of the moment is both heady and terrifying.

I want to tell him. About me. About everything. I want to rip my heart out of my chest and hand it to him so he can see the scars and heal them with his doctor's touch.

But I don't because my heart is like his knee. It functions, but no amount of care will ever make it what it was. There's no going back to the start. The ghosts of my past will not be buried. I can't close my eyes, play naïve, and hope my wolves won't be caught in the crossfire. Not anymore.

The realization strips me from this sense of humanity and wholesomeness I've only just found again, but there's no other choice. It will destroy me, but I must leave them.

And soon.

ANNA SUN

SAM

"*P*repare to wolf-up, Sam. We have uninvited guests," Dom announces with a raised voice, shattering the *post-night-of-passion* 1:00 am snack.

I reluctantly untangle my hands from Vicky's hair and place one last kiss on her neck before craning my neck around to Dominic.

His eyes are torn between the emergency he's come to warn me about and the urge to tease me for my nakedness. "I see you're ready to head out," he chuckles, motioning to my bare ass.

I roll my eyes and grab my jeans on the back of the couch, pulling them up in a hurry.

Dom sobers up, his bad-news face back in full force. "There are three separate vamp trails stinking up the woods near the highway."

Vicky's lips quiver, and a full-bodied shiver brands her. "He found me," she says on a shuddering breath, a bottomless agony lacing the word. She swallows, pushes her plate aside, and nods. The movements possess a strange sense of abdication and acceptance. Like she expected this and is coming to terms with the consequences. Like she's okay with it being the end.

My heart hammers in my chest.

Not only didn't I follow Gabriel's advice not to fall for her, I tripped over my heart and landed flat on my face. The love swirling in my veins, in my bones, is scary and all-consuming because it's not yet fixed into years and years of trust and dependability. She's made no promises, but I'll die if she leaves me. She's the cure for my numbness, the adventure Dom craves, and, even if he still won't admit it, the perfect match to Gabriel's fire.

She is everything.

Toast crumbs fall off her hands when she dusts them off and stands.

Dom catches up. "You're just going to bolt?"

"I come. I see. I fuck the hottest men around, and then move on. It's what I do," she says nonchalantly.

My stomach rolls, and I'm about to give her hell for her hypocrisy when I notice her knees are shaking.

I chase after her and wrap my arm around her shoulders from behind. "Who's after you?"

Her beautiful red lips stretch in a thin smile. She twists in my arms and cups my face. "Maybe I'll see you around, Sam."

See you around? How the hell does *see you around* follow the most perfect night of my life? "Who's after you?" My tone is hardened by the goodbye written across her face. If she thinks we'll let her leave without a word of explanation, she's dreaming.

"You wouldn't know him," she says.

Dom grips her waist from behind. "I know he's a vamp. They don't have business on our turf."

She bites her bottom lip. "He's powerful and dangerous. The last thing I want is to bring you guys into this mess. You've got your own problems."

"Stay. We'll protect you," I whisper.

"You can't," she insists.

Dom nibbles her neck. "We're tough."

A melodic chuckle pops out of her mouth. "I know." She smiles, but it's not the same one I'm used to. It's too... calculated. "I've had a lot of *fun* with you guys."

Dom strokes her sides. "Come on, baby. Tell us the truth. You belong here."

Something eerie passes in her eyes, and her jaw clenches. "I do not belong to you. Or anyone. If I want to leave, it's my business." She shoves us off and disappears inside my room.

Fear stinks up the air in her wake.

Dom and I exchange a look.

"She's afraid," he says.

"Very."

"We're not letting her go, are we?"

"Nope."

When she returns, fully dressed, Dom crouches in front of the door, his feet digging into the floor.

She huffs, "Are you kidding? Move."

He flashes her a wicked smile. "No."

"Sam, talk to him."

I shake my head. "I'm not letting you out of my sight. Not until you tell us what's wrong."

"The second Gabe orders you to let me go, you'll have to obey."

Silence falls over the scene, and Gabriel's booming voice resonates across the room. "Too bad for you; I agree with them." Our alpha climbs the stairs with a dark expression on his face.

Vicky whips around and gawks.

His gray eyes bear into us all in turn, smothering with a blinding thirst for blood. "First, we'll hunt those vampires and dust them. Then, we're all going to sit around this table, and you'll tell us why they're willing to risk their skins to get you back. That's an order."

Dom smirks, and the tight knot my chest eases. For once, Dom, Gabe and I are all on the same page.

MY FIRST KISS

VICKY

A silver stream of mist hangs from the pines' lower branches. The clouds above reap the light of the moon, opaque darkness making the forest seem narrower. Thankfully, my demonic eyesight is only mildly bothered by the lack of light. Dom hops over a large inverted trunk, his white fur like a beacon in the night.

Sam ran ahead with Gabriel. Their plan is to capture one vampire, so they can interrogate him, and kill the rest. My plan is to take no prisoners. I can't have a vamp babbling my real identity to my wolves.

I wonder if it's the Pereiras, looking for their dead, or Ludovic's men. I'm not fooling myself thinking one option is really better than the other. Whoever is canvassing the woods will be followed by a new batch, then another. As long as I'm here, they will keep coming.

Dom sniffs the air, his paws digging in the earth.

Quick footsteps reach my ears over the rustling of the wind, and I face the direction from which they are coming.

When my wolf breaks into a run, I try to catch up, but he swerves around the pines like a slalom champion. A big hill looms in front of me. I hear growls, the dry rip of fabric and push my legs to their limit. The steep terrain slows my ascension, my lungs burning.

Almost there.

A heart-breaking animal cry resonates deep in my chest, and I choke on a rushed breath. The sickening bone-snapping sound that comes next echoes around the trees.

Dom is sprawled on the ground at the bottom of a large oak. An imposing shadow crouches above him.

"Don't hurt him, or I'll slice your head off!" I scream, raising my sword.

The silhouette pivots toward me, its feline grace thickening my blood. The vampire has got one hand wrapped around Dom's throat.

Wait a minute... I know those shoulders.

"I thought Ludovic was going mad, but it is you," a velvety voice says.

Alec Beaumont, the deadliest member of the king's guard, is here, his signature garnet eyes fixed on me.

My grip falters. This isn't a random sweep. This is James Bond with a license to kill. Red lines slither across the turn-down collar of his undershirt, and his expensive jacket is ripped.

"Alec. Hi." I force some warmth into my voice.

"What the fuck are you doing with wolves, Elle?"

The nickname reminds me that we used to be friends, and acid rises to my mouth.

Once upon a time, he had a massive crush on me. I even thought he loved me. Maybe there's a deal to be made here. "Let's talk about this."

He jerks his hand off Dominic and stands tall. "There's nothing to *talk* about. You think it was bad when you lived at court? It's ten times worse now. Ludovic will not let any of us breathe until you are returned to him."

Should I attack? Should I not? Saving Dom's life is more important. If I miss, it'd be too easy for Alec to finish him off.

"What if I disappeared again?" I croak, bridging the gap between us.

Alec shakes his head. "It won't work this time. If I come back empty handed, he'll have me rally the troops."

I take my chances and strike him, aiming for his throat. He knocks the weapon out of my hand and turns it on me.

The pointy end scrapes the hollow of my neck.

Alec steps back. "You think I want to murder a village filled with women and children? I don't. But I'll be forced to, if you're not reasonable." He flings my blade to the ground, and the handle digs into the soft earth. "I'll give you one day. Finish whatever this is and meet me there tomorrow," he hands me a piece of paper. "I'll keep this town's existence a secret."

I read the address and memorize it.

He shrugs off his torn jacket and hikes his sleeves up. "If you don't come—"

"I will." I hear footsteps closing in on us and snatch my blade from the ground. "What about the others?"

Alec peers at the darkness smothering us. "They're not mine. Pereira sent his mercenaries, and their leader is a real prick. He wants to be the one to turn you in. I can't vouch for what they'll do."

My grip tightens on the sword's hilt. "I'll take care of them."

He eyes my weapon, his brows raised. "You've changed, Elle."

"For the better." My cheeks sear in shame at the memory of who I used to be. Eleanor was weak. Easily manipulated. Cruel and dreadfully unhappy. I wave Alec away with a growl. "Go. I'll see you tomorrow."

"No later than midnight, Cinderella." He dashes out, leaving me upwind of the other vampires.

They don't intimidate me as much as Alec does, but guarding a bloody wolf while fighting off vamps is a tall order.

Four soldiers prowl out of the shadows and surround me. They are wearing dark jeans and T-shirts like they suddenly decided to hunt me down before going to the movies. Like they don't take this seriously at all.

Standing my ground, I rise my blade into the air. They all come at me at the same time. The first head rolls to my feet and explodes into dust.

The other three jerk back in surprise. One of them shoots me in the back. A sharp sting throbs all the way up my spine to my head, my pulse echoing at my temples.

I lunge at the shooter, slicing his neck off in a clean swipe.

A dagger sinks into my shoulder. Gritting my teeth, I close my hands around the hilt and pry it out. There's no aconite coating the blade, so it should heal quickly, but my arm is limp in the meantime.

I pick up the sword with my other hand and strike the air, holding the vampires at bay.

When a second projectile pierces my stomach, I stagger. At this rate, I'll have more holes than a colander. "You need me alive."

The dark-skinned one twirls his sword around his wrist. "Alive, yes. In good shape? No."

Another round bites into my flesh, and he attacks. I try to parry, but my nerves are screaming in agony, and he knocks me down to my ass.

My visions blurs as the fucker sinks the tip of his blade in my belly. Blood pours out of the wound, and he kneels next to me with the biggest smirk on his face. "Whoops. Looks like I won."

A huge black wolf stalks from the shadows. It's got at least 50 pounds on Dom, and at once I recognize Gabriel's stern predatory stare. He launches himself high in the air, landing directly on the vampire's back. Gabe tears out my attacker's neck with his big jaw. The body turns to dust, leaving fabric and a belt behind.

I crawl next to Dom and check his pulse. His fur is all sticky with blood, but he's alive.

The last vampire shoots incessantly at Gabriel, but the wolf tackles him to the ground and mauls his arm off before delivering the killing blow.

Death and smoke hang in the air, the alpha's breaths slowly returning to normal.

The black fur swells and melts into skin as Gabe changes back into his human form. I gawk at his naked ass before he pulls one of the dusted vamps' pants on, the fabric straining against his large thighs. He combs his messy hair back. "Is the kid..."

I bend over Dom's wolf form, checking his breathing again. "He's alive."

"Billie got hurt, too. Sam took her back to the cabin." Blood stains Gabriel's face and neck. "You dusted two of them? These vampires were twice your size and weight."

"And slower and dumber for it."

He checks on Dom. "Still. You should have let us deal with them."

"Please. Soon, you'll be telling me my place is in the kitchen."

"My choices are gruesome brawls or *the kitchen*?" He shakes his head. "I'll bring Dominic home first and come back for you."

"Okay." I straighten up, and pain slithers across my belly.

Gabriel frowns. "Show me." He pries my hands away from my stomach with a low hiss. "He almost ran you through."

Sweat pearls on my forehead. "I'm fine."

"You'll bleed out if you're not careful." He presses the dead vampire's shirt to my wound to slow the bleeding, but the trickle intensifies.

I realize he's right. "I need a boost. Kiss me."

His fists curl, his face and thoughts veiled in shadows. "No."

"Afraid to feel something? It's a kiss, not a proposal. It'll help me heal."

He clicks his tongue. "Just this once."

My heart is beating like a drum. Thump. Thump. *Thump*.

Knees in the dirt, Gabriel shuffles closer to me and cradles my face in his big hands. I feel light-headed. Could be the blood loss.

Could be Gabriel's gray eyes pulsing with something foreign and suffocating as he leans in to kiss me.

Rough lips, silky breaths, and a pinch of sea salt.

His energy packs a serious power-up, and I'm dizzy. I don't even feel that stab wound anymore. But what knocks me out completely is the brush of his tongue against mine.

He groans against my mouth before deepening the kiss, his hands tangled in my hair. He starts slow, controlled, as if he's only performing a task, but soon the rhythm accelerates.

His talented mouth ravishes me twist after twist, graze after graze, kiss after kiss.

It's like he wants to punish me for forcing this on him. Or punish himself for liking it.

The back of my head presses against the ground, my arms flying around his neck.

All these weeks of telling myself I wasn't *that* into Gabriel.

What a joke.

He's the embodiment of power and strength, but with a nice dose of humanity. He loves his people and would gladly give his life for them. He's both a never-ending storm and an immutable rock. And boy... I would love to be caught in that storm long enough to wash up against him.

The alpha pulls away, but I'm too breathless to move.

"Let's *never* do that again," he chucks out, rising to his feet.

And I whimper, because I'd been thinking the exact opposite.

ALREADY GONE

VICKY

"These were trained soldiers." Dom turns to me for an explanation, his broken arm in a splint, a big bruise on his head.

Sam said he should recover in about a day, but I still feel awful. My heart is beating in my throat. "I pissed off the wrong vampire, I guess."

"You promised to tell us the truth," the young wolf whines.

Not really, but I prefer not to point that out. "We'll hash this out later."

Gabriel's kiss sped up my recovery better than I could have hoped, and Sam only had to dig out one bullet out of my back. The other holes and the stab wound are already healed.

Billie wobbles out of Sam's exam room with fresh stitches on her wrist.

Gabriel strolls to her and places a hand at the small of her back. "You okay?" There's a softness to his voice that I haven't heard often.

"You know me. Always up for a fight." She tucks a brown lock behind her ears.

"Come. I'll drive you home," the alpha says.

A bright blush colors her chest, and she takes his offered arm.

It surprises me that he involved her in my vampire mess, but maybe they're growing closer.

Sam ushers me to Dom's room, and I lie between them on our bed. My eyes scan the injured wolf every few minutes to make sure he's doing okay. I hang onto consciousness for as long as I can. I want to imprint their faces, their warmth, even the sweet rumble of their light snores in my memory.

We sleep the day away, and when Gabriel wakes us up around 4 pm, my head is pounding.

The alpha gives me a pointed glare from the doorway. "There's a mixer in town tonight to introduce the new recruits. Our conversation will have to wait until tomorrow, but don't kid yourself thinking I'll forget."

Tomorrow... I guess I'll spare myself the wretched discussion after all. I wish I could tell them the truth before I go, but I don't want to risk a volatile reaction from Gabriel. And Dom will never accept my reasons. They are better off if I leave and don't look back.

I rub my crusty eyes. "A mixer? Am I invited?" It's my last night... might as well make it fun.

Gabe's jaw twitches. "I suppose." His shoulders are stiff as hell, and he walks away. He's still pissed about the kiss.

Sam and Dom's gazes weigh heavily on me.

I climb over Sam and hop to my feet. "So... a mixer. Do I get to see you both in a suit?" I wiggle my eyebrows at them.

Dom points to his injured arm. "I'll use this as an excuse not to dress up."

Sam stretches gingerly. "I'll wear a suit."

I lick my lips in anticipation. "I'll call Lena."

I end up borrowing a dress from her friend Jenny and join the guys at the school. The gym is apparently the only reception hall, so it feels like going to prom. Balloons and ribbons greet us by the door, and I decide to treat tonight as my unofficial going-away party.

The whole town is here. Lena explained that the attendance is mandatory for anyone over 18. It's a pack thing. They have to make sure the new wolves will mesh well and weed out potential trouble elements.

There are at least three hundred shifters chatting and sipping on drinks. Many females are all dolled-up, probably eager to sample the new wolf-goods.

Gabriel glowers when he sees me coming in with Lena.

"Gabe hates that we're friends," I whisper in her ear, and we each snatch a flute of champagne from the bar.

"My dad doesn't want me talking to you either. Fuck them."

I raise my glass.

Dominic joins us by the dance floor. "That dress is sinful. Red? It's a wolf's dream."

I peek over my shoulder to the plunging back of my dress. "You like it?"

"I *love* it." The way his voice lowers at the word *love* drums in my chest. I'll miss Dom the most, I think. I'll miss how... effortless everything is when I'm with him.

Sam appears from behind and offers me his hand. "Can I have this dance?"

The doctor's curls are expertly gelled for the occasion, his suit highlighting his tall but muscular frame. We sway to the smooth music, and I rest my head on his chest. His cologne is to die for, the musky scent tingling in my belly.

One of the nasty women from the grocery store is slow dancing with a tall man directly behind Sam, and I wink at her when our gazes meet. She scowls, but from the way her partner is caressing the small of her back, I'm sure she doesn't have eyes for Sam anymore.

He twirls me around, and I giggle before he crushes me to him, the outline of his chest and thighs pressing against me. He's hard.

No, I'll miss Sam the most. He's a one-in-a-million kind of man.

Breathtakingly sweet and fuck-hot at the same time. I could have stared at his blue eyes for centuries.

"Can I cut in for a sec?" Gabriel asks, the low baritone rippling across my wary heart.

Sam blushes and discreetly adjusts his pants before handing me over to his alpha.

Gabriel's gaze skims my curves. "That's...quite a dress."

"Thank you."

Our hips touch. He doesn't crush me to him or hold me at an awkward distance. No, it's a perfectly polite and casual hold, and I'm reminded again that he's completely unaffected by my powers—and my body. He's the only man who's ever slow danced with me like I'm slightly annoying but perfectly harmless. And I hate it.

I tremble when his thumb caresses the V-shaped fabric at my lower back, and our eyes meet.

Gabriel stops moving, the sea of swaying bodies continuing without us. I shiver under the intense stare, his dark eyes prying away all my secrets. It's like he knows what I'm planning. I half-expect him to say goodbye. His gaze darts to the side, and he nods in my general direction before walking away.

I exhale.

Was that it? Was that his blessing? Or am I reading too much into a minute-long dance?

I'll miss him too. There'll always be a big question mark right next to his name. What if I'd stayed longer? What if he'd let me crawl under his skin? I'll always feel like I missed out on something with him.

Lena and I dance with the younger crowd. We drink, we laugh. It's a nice way to say goodbye.

Dom strolls over to me. "As much as it *kills* me to miss this." He motions to my dress. "My head is about to explode. I'm going to pop a lot of sleeping pills and crash. Rain check?"

I'll never see him again, and the realization punches my heart like a fist. Standing on the tip of my toes, I kiss him hard.

He groans into my mouth, his hips tilting into mine. "What was that for?"

I sink my nails in my palms and force a smile on my face. "Your sexy wound."

"I'll need a nurse tomorrow." He runs his nose up the slope of my neck.

The gentle graze tearing out what's left of my courage, and the corners of my mouth hurt. "Tomorrow."

Dominic walks away with a wink, and the sting in my eyes burns a fiery path down my throat. What the fuck? I don't do tears.

Lena approaches, oblivious. She points to the dance floor. "Check it out. Billie roped Gabe into dancing with her."

Billie is wearing a sexy black dress, the expression in her eyes leaving me no doubt she planned her night well. I can't see Gabriel's face from where we're standing, but he looks like he's enjoying himself. He's not holding *her* like she's perfectly harmless.

They head off the dance floor together, Billie tugging on his arm.

"I think Billie is getting lucky tonight," Lena enunciates slowly.

I force another painful smile on my face and smack myself inwardly for being so disappointed. We're somewhat friends now. It's ions better than what we were before, and it's enough.

It makes no difference since I'm leaving.

God. The twinkling lights of the dance floor shine into a wet blotch, the tears veiling my vision and making everything blurry.

Well... not everything. Some things are clearer than ever.

I was happy here.

I had Sam and Dom.

Love, laughs, mind-blowing sex.

I had an actual girlfriend—a friend who's a girl and who's not a vandella.

I could have built something that would have amounted to more than an endless string of lovers.

But it was a dream. A beautiful, fleeting fairy tale.

Sam wraps his arms around me from behind and kisses the back of my ear. I lean into him. The contrast between his hard chest and his soft breath melts my insides.

"Bad news. I have to patrol tonight in Dom's place. You'll be okay?"

I rake my fingertips across the gentle, beautiful hand resting on my stomach. "I'm great. Lena will drive me home."

I'll head to the cabin, change, and disappear into the night. The prospect nearly makes me gag, a big lump crushing my airways.

Love is a poisoned apple.

INTO THE OCEAN

VICKY

*M*y hand grips the top of the banister, and I pry off my heels over the scratchy doormat by the staircase. The lights are off, the living room and kitchen wrapped in darkness. I slip my feet into my sneakers and freeze.

The door leading to Gabe's room is ajar. He's uptight about his damn privacy, but he's definitely not coming home for a while. Where's the harm in a last-minute snooping excursion? If he smells my trail, he can lash out at my ghost.

Will I haunt my wolves' dreams for a while, or will my memory be tossed out with the weekly thrash? Will they suspect the depths of my feelings for them or write me off as an ill-advised fling?

I guess I'll never know.

The steps creak under my soles. Hand shaking, I flip open the switch to Gabriel's world.

There's a king-sized bed, a dresser, and a bathroom in the corner. It's grand and frugal all at once, but the thing that catches my attention is the huge freezer right by the entrance. It's one of those industrial deep-freeze units, and there's a generator right alongside it.

Why would Gabriel keep an industrial freezer in his bedroom?

I crack open the latch, expecting nothing short of a body, but the big freezer is filled with blood bags. Hundreds of them. Sam's meticulous handwriting is on all of them, the stickers displaying the date and the letter G. What the hell? I used to be married to a vampire, but never before have I seen so many snack-portions of blood in the same place. It makes no sense... why would Gabe keep those here?

I scan the room for clues, but Gabriel is clearly OCD with his stuff, the surfaces squeaky clean and barren.

Except for one thing.

There's a black-and-white photograph on his dresser, and I pick it up, stunned. The young woman is sitting in the back of an old pickup truck, her dress and long blond hair flowing in the wind. Her smile is blinding, and though I've only seen this woman once before, in a different photograph, I can easily recognize her. It also helps that Lena is the spitting image of her mother.

I flip the frame around. June, Summer 1941. There's an old letter tucked in the corner, and I unfold it.

I love you, always...

June

Gabriel was in love with Lena's mother?

And then, it clicks. The blood storage. Lena's sickness. Gabriel's intense warnings that I should stay away from her...

Holy shit!

"Little red riding hood walked right into the wolf's mouth."

My pulse spikes at the low drag of Gabriel's voice. Busted.

Any joy at the knowledge that he didn't take Billie home is quickly smothered by fear. He pushes me deeper into the room and waves his arms around like he's welcoming me into his lair. "How long have you been here? One minute? Two?" He leans towards the freezer and sniffs the air. "You figured out my secret."

"What secret?"

His teeth grit together. "Don't play with me."

Saliva balls into a painful boulder in my throat. "You're Lena's father."

"Yes." The word is quiet. Deadly.

I inch away from him and drop the picture frame. It falls to the ground with a thud.

Before I can blink, Gabriel flattens me to the wall face-first, his arms caging me in. I wait for the blow I'm sure is coming. He can't trust me to keep his secret, so he'll do the next best thing. Kill me. Will he choke me to death? Snap my neck?

My heart pounds in a fast, rough rhythm while I wait.

And wait.

And wait.

His breaths weigh heavily on my shoulder. "These four walls belong only to me. Out there, I have to be their leader, their priest, their father, their fucking God. I'm the asshole who orders them around, keeps them safe, and makes the hard decisions." He takes a long pause. "But in here... in here I can be whoever the fuck I want. Do you understand the difference?"

I swallow hard and nod, and he gives me an inch to spare. I start twisting around to look at his face, to see if my death sentence is confirmed.

He grips my neck. "I'm not done. Face the wall and listen." His thumb grazes my hairline. The touch is strangely gentle. "In here, I don't have to be my best. I can be weak."

My breath stutters in my chest. *Weak?* A full-on gasp escapes me when Gabriel slides his hand down my spine and palms my ass over my red dress.

"I can admit that I've been dying to fuck the annoyingly beautiful she-demon who taunts me day and night."

Heat pools in my belly, my fears veiled by a new, potent longing. My already violent heartbeats climb to my throat. The dark paint is cold under my touch as I brace my arms against the wall not to lose my balance.

His chest molds against my back, and he pushes his hips into me, showing me the extent of his need. "I don't have to hide how hard I am for her. To deny that I touch myself to her moans while another man pleasures her, giving her what she wants, but not what she needs. I can say how badly I want to rip her clothes off and hear her scream *my* name."

A wild shiver quakes my body at the sound of his zipper, and I freeze. This is moving fast. "What if I say no?"

A dark chuckle stirs the hairs on my neck. "You're not going to say no."

That prick. He's right. My cheeks heat up. My underwear is already soaked through, the heady scent of arousal and sweat probably multiplied tenfold in his wolf nose.

He caresses the side of my thigh from my knee to my hips, hiking my dress up in the process, and I arch into him.

His big hand slips beneath the elastic of my thong. The fabric bites into my flesh before it rips, and he dips his tongue in the hollow behind my ear. "Will you scream for me, Blondie?"

He stretches my neckline down. My breasts spring free, and I hold my breath. The heat of his hands feels amazing as he plays with them, pinching and flicking my nipples like they exist solely to please him. "They're all jealous of your tits..." He kneels down behind me. "But every woman in this town hates you because of that ass."

I yelp as he bites me, but it's a superficial nip.

His nose bumps against the back of my thighs, and two fingers sink inside my heat. "Are you that wet for them?"

I groan, my head falling forward, and rub myself against him, the pulsing ache between my legs making my head spin.

"So needy..." Trailing his fingers up my slippery thighs, he gathers the arousal dripping down the skin.

He stands and grazes my bottom lip with his index finger, and I suck it inside my mouth, the salty taste of my desire making my lids flutter.

The smooth head of his shaft drags across my ass. "Beg for it. Beg for my cock."

"Stop fucking around and take me!"

The flavor of his lust is different. It's steady and powerful, but I can't tap into his energy.

His hands settle on my hipbones. "You can't feed off me unless I want you to." His broad tip nudges my entrance. "I've done my homework." The wicked dance continues. He moves one hand to taunt my nipples, palming my breast before inching down with insidious slowness to my sex.

I arch my butt up. I need him to stop this. To stop reminding me that he's not aching for me as badly as I am aching for him.

"Beg, Blondie." He leisurely parts my suffering folds with one cruel finger that isn't big or hard enough to heal my pain. My molten core beats with need.

"Please, Gabriel. Please, please, please."

He finally gives me what I need, crashing inside me with one hard stroke, and I cry out. The pleasure is sharp and heavy. His thick, uncompromising length stretches my flesh. The tight muscles should sting, but my swollen walls are drenched and allow for both his passion and girth.

"Yes!" I shout, dazed by the exquisite tension.

He fucks me to own me, and in that moment, he does.

I'm both thrilled and terrified by how good it feels. There's a darkness inside my soul that rises to the challenge and hungers for more. I've been smothering this spark for years, letting it flicker into nothingness. Now that it burns bright again, it chars me with its heat, scorching me, savage and beautiful.

The intricate tangle of pleasure and agony finally explodes across my nerve endings, and I scream. It's so acute I'm vibrating, my whole body clenching in a release so intense that I'm gasping for breath.

Gabriel steadies me through the storm until he's sure I won't topple over.

Using my climax as lube, he rubs himself along the path to my ass.

"You're all about the ass," I tease, shying away from the intensity of the moment.

"I won't apologize for what I like." He nicks my ear with his teeth. "Can you handle it?"

It's been forever since... but I used to like it. Fuck, I used to like it a lot. "Yes!"

"Good answer." He preps me with a few gentle pushes until I relax enough to take him all in. "Ah, fuck, fuck, fuck."

A heated pride swells in my chest. "Too much for you?"

A hard breath flutters down my neck, and he holds me to him, barely moving like he's about to blow.

I want to rock his socks off so he never forgets me. He needs to let go of his perfect alpha control first, so I spread my legs, taking him even deeper. His rock-hard chest presses into my back.

Soft kisses melt like snowflakes over my shoulders.

Gabriel sucks my earlobe into his mouth. "Touch yourself. I want you to come with my cock deep in your ass."

I'm all for it and give my swollen lips a few flicks while Gabe defiles my breasts again. He drags in and out, deeper and deeper. His ragged breaths and low curses are fucking music to my ears.

My walls quiver around my fingers, and the alpha's hunger is palpable in his rough handling of my hips and the unrestrained intensity of his thrusts.

I touch him through my back wall, and his hips buck. "You're a witch." I feel him throb inside me, but he pulls out.

His hot release slashes across my ass, branding me, before he tears my dress off my back.

"Undressing me after sex? Seems like a waste."

"I'll have to burn the damn thing." He catches his breath, his strong hold preventing me from turning around to face him. "Listen carefully, Blondie. I'm going to walk right into my bathroom over there." He points to the back. "When I return, you will be gone. You'll go upstairs, shower my scent off you, and we'll never talk about this again."

"Yes, sir," I breathe, half-serious, half-taunting.

He growls and stalks off to his bathroom.

I was wrong before; he has no idea that this was our last conversation.

WILD HEARTS CAN'T BE BROKEN

VICKY

I reach the edge of town in Sam's Jeep. It's the same place I was stopped by Gabriel's man last time, and I watch for signs of a patrol. If everyone is at the dance, this is the perfect time to escape. The spiked tire-shredders have been moved a few feet to the left, allowing for a car to pass. Acid simmers at the back of my throat, but I can't chicken out now. This is it. I'm leaving. Forever.

A terrifying shiver rattles my ribcage, and I press the accelerator down.

The regional road is empty, and my heartbeats drum deep in my chest. Fifteen minutes later, I merge onto the highway and speed up.

A loud exhale escapes me when I spot Lena's small Toyota a few hundred feet in front of me, the white Snoopy sticker gleaming in the night. Why is she sneaking out of town? What is she thinking?

She takes the next exit, and I glance at the clock. It's only 10:46 pm. I have time.

"What are you doing here, Lena?" I shout out loud, following her car. There might be vampires crawling around these parts. Does she want to be taken hostage? Even if she doesn't know she's Gabriel's daughter, she must realize how reckless this is.

The Toyota pulls into a gas station, and I park a few feet behind it. Hand on the doorknob, I'm about to hop out when a silhouette climbs out of the car. The tall man looks too big for the tiny car and stretches his legs. It's Jeff, Lena's dad. A woman with long brown hair jumps to her feet on the passenger side. It's not Lena. I feel stupid and wrench the stick shift into reverse. The woman's face catches the floodlights of the overhead canopy, and my stomach lurches, my feet cramping on the brakes.

It's Evelyn—as in Gabriel's ex-wife. With Jeff.

Fuck.

Without giving myself too much time to think it through, I yank my hoodie over my head, park at the pump at the very back of the station, and eavesdrop.

"Fill it to the brim. We're not stopping again until we get to Portland," Evelyn says before walking toward the building.

Jeff tucks the nozzle into the tank.

And then I hear a groan. A faint, whiny sound followed by muffled thumps. A human would never have picked up on it, but I hear it. Ice slithers inside my heart, and I steal a glance at the Toyota's trunk.

There's someone inside, probably gagged by the choked whimpers, trying to beat her way out.

Lena.

I jump back into the Jeep, and my fingers fumble over my phone's screen. I hit Gabriel's number. The shrill dial tone whips my frenzy up with each beep.

Pick up. Pick up. Pick up.

"Where are you calling from? Upstairs?" He barks, and I know he almost didn't answer.

"I'm not upstairs. It's about Lena, Gabriel." I have his attention now, perfect silence falling over the line. "I followed her car to a big gas station off the highway near exit 18."

"What the fuck is she doing there?" His words are rough, but he's breathless.

"It's her dad. And Evelyn. They are here together, and I think—I think Lena's bound in the trunk. I heard them say they're heading for Portland."

"Please follow them," his voice is incredibly dark and impossibly low.

I nod, my mouth dry. "I will."

"I'll call you back in five minutes."

Jeff and Evelyn return to the highway. I stay a couple of cars behind them, trying to be discrete, and memorize the signs we cross.

When Gabriel calls back, I report everything in detail.

He's in his car, the rumble of the engine audible behind him. "A friend of mine will set up a police roadblock about twenty minutes in front of you. I'm twenty behind, but I'll catch up quickly."

"Did you bring Sam?"

"I'm alone. Sam is patrolling and Dom is not fit for duty. This thing... it shouldn't get out." There's a pregnant pause. "I'll see you soon. Call if they change course."

"I will."

We hang up.

Just as Gabriel explained, the cars grind to a halt about twenty minutes later.

Red and blue sirens flash over the stopped traffic, and I roll the window open wide. Lena's car is in the other lane, separated from mine by a delivery truck and a Camry. There are about eight cars in front of them.

Evelyn steps out and peers at the roadblock.

A policeman walks towards the first rows of cars and speaks to the drivers, then the next. He reaches Evelyn and chats with her for a bit. She gets back inside her car, and the policeman continues until he's standing next to my window.

"Bad accident, Ma'am, but we're almost ready to let people through." Our eyes meet, and he leans closer. "Vicky?"

"Yes."

"Gabriel will be here in fifteen minutes. I stopped traffic behind you, and I'll let as many of the civilians as I can go around us right as he's about to get here, but we'll have to deal with the rest."

I nod.

He returns to his car.

My palms are sweaty. It's 11:19, and I already passed Alec's rendezvous point. I could be back there in fifteen minutes if I hurried. There's still time.

I gnaw half my fingers off waiting for Gabriel to arrive.

When one of the police car slides to the side and lets people through one by one, my pulse surges. Jeff starts the Toyota and inches forward.

Gabriel's black truck screeches to a halt directly behind me.

Whirls of smoke rise from the back tires of the Toyota. Jeff drives at full-speed toward the narrow passage, but a big armored car blocks his escape. He and Evelyn jolt out of the car and start shooting at the policemen.

Screams of panic resonate around us, and I slide out of the Jeep, making sure I'm well covered. A high, buzzing sound squeaks into my ears when Jeff turns his gun on Gabriel. I peek over the bumper and see Evelyn take one bullet square in her shoulder. She staggers to her knees.

Gabriel dashes closer to them, his gun still held high. "It's over, Jeff."

"You're right about that." Lena's dad aims at Gabriel's head.

The alpha shoots the weapon out of Jeff's hand, disarming him with one perfect shot. "If Lena's in the trunk, you're a dead man."

Jeff holds his bleeding hand to his chest. "Suddenly, you care about her? Where were you when she was born? When she had her tonsils removed? When she cried on the first day of school? She's *my* daughter, Gabriel."

Gabe's gaze darts from his ex-wife to the man that betrayed him. "How long have you known?"

"When Lena got sick, I connected the dots. Why would *your* blood be the cure? Sam made up a good story, but I'm not that stupid." He motions to his accomplice. "Evelyn confirmed it. You fucked my wife for how many decades?"

Gabriel's traits harden. "She was mine long before she was yours. I knew her as June Weston."

"Liar! Her parents didn't bring her here until the end of the war."

"I was an idiot for not marrying her before I left. I came back from the war three years too late with a pup in tow and begged her to break with you. But you'd already bitten her, and she didn't want to condemn you to an empty life. She chose you, Dawson," Gabriel says, disgust and disappointment rolling off his tongue.

Jeff spits on the ground. "She still betrayed me."

"The third miscarriage hit her hard. She came to me, desperate for company after you ran off on another drinking binge. Lena was a miracle. It felt like the universe was offering us a second chance. But again, she chose you. And I honored that choice, pulled you from active duty and let you raise *my* daughter." Gabriel points his gun at Evelyn. "Open the trunk."

She inches to the driver's side. "You only ever loved her. You never should have married me." Blood streams down her arm as she pulls on the lever.

"That's true," Gabe admits. "Still... you cheated on me for a year with my best lieutenant, so excuse me for not feeling guilty."

Lena's dark waves and blue highlights appear. She's fighting against her restraints, and I run over to her. Her face is wide with fear and shock. After I free her hands, she claws the gag off her mouth. A throng of questions swirl in her red-rimmed eyes. I watch her face and her beautiful long black hair and see the resemblance. It's not so pronounced that it's obvious, but now that I know, it makes so much sense. They have the same proud nose, the same effortless grace. I help her to her feet, and she quivers, walking between the two men.

She gives Gabriel a haunted look. "You're my father?"

The alpha swallows hard.

She turns to Jeff. "Dad?" She squeaks like she wants him to deny it.

"He's your biological father, but I'll always be your dad," Jeff breathes.

"And you're the one—the one who betrayed the pack?" Lena's features are torn open by raw pain and horror.

"I did it for you, honey."

She presses a hand to her mouth like she's about to barf.

He reaches for her, but she staggers backwards and closer to Gabriel and me.

"Sweetpea, be reasonable. You always wanted to get out of here," Jeff begs.

"If you were so sure I wanted to leave, why did you tie me up and toss me in the trunk?"

"There was no time to explain."

"All these questions. About Gabriel. About Vicky. You weren't worried about me. You were using me to spy on them." Lena screws her eyes shut, tears streaking down her heated cheeks. "Go!"

"Lena..."

"I said go!"

"I can't let—" Gabriel starts.

Lena grits her teeth. "But you will."

I sink my nails into Gabriel's arm. He has to let them go. He can't kill Lena's Dad if he wants to keep her. The war general and the father battle over what to do.

When he finally lowers his gun, I exhale deep.

"Go. But if you ever set foot back in Oregon, I won't be lenient again," he seethes.

I wrap my arm around Lena and hold her to my side. Gabriel's police friend deals with the civilians while Lena cries on my shoulder. I usher her in the back of the Jeep and Gabriel hops in the driver seat. His truck has a flat tire.

A boulder of nerves knocks the wind out of me, the car's clock glaring at me from the dashboard.

12:18 am.

Cinderella is beyond late.

I know Alec wasn't kidding about the steep deadline. He'll be on his way to Europe so he can rally an army and storm this town. Since his solo extraction mission failed, Alec will not botch this. By my calculations, it'll take at least ten days for him to prepare a wide-scale attack.

I'll spend a few more greedy days with my wolves before flying to Canada or Mexico. If I'm no longer here, Alec will leave them alone. He has no reason to believe this was more than a convenient place to hide. If I attract enough attention and maybe make a public spectacle, he'll come after me, not them. I'll think of something.

We drive back to the cabin.

Lena crashes in Sam's room for the night. The poor girl is in shock and asks for privacy.

"How did you figure it out?" Gabriel asks once we're alone. Deep lines crease the alpha's forehead, and he passes a tired hand over his features.

I wish I could kiss the frown off his face. "I drove back to the party and saw Lena's car heading out of town. I got curious and followed. It wasn't until Jeff stopped at the gas station that I realized what was happening." It's only half a lie.

"Thank God you followed them." The *thank you* resonating across each word warms my chest. He wipes his big hand over his face and strolls downstairs, his shoulders hunched.

I sneak into Dom's bed, the light snores coming from him making me smile, and bury my face in his back. Bark, fresh pine needles and a hint of sweat fill my lungs.

He stirs when I trace his arm. "Are you okay?"

"Yeah." I'm better than okay. I've got more time with them. Just a little more time.

"Hey," Sam says from the door. "Can I impose?" He slips under the covers on the other side of me and places a soft kiss at the nape of my neck. "Lena knows."

"Yes."

"What happened?" Dom asks.

I recount the events of the night to my wolves. All but the sex, of course.

"I can't believe I didn't know," Dom whispers.

Sam's face twists with guilt. "Sorry. Gabe swore me to secrecy."

"I understand."

I dose off with Sam's hands on my stomach and Dom's goodnight kiss brushing my lips, and I'm too tired to remind myself that it's only borrowed time.

Too tired to mourn this life that was just beginning.

SLOW DANCING IN A BURNING ROOM

VICKY

"*I* didn't go with him, but I didn't do it for you," Lena declares the next morning.

We're all sitting around the island eating breakfast, and her outburst takes everyone by surprise.

Dom drops his fork, and Sam loses a few inches, his eyes now glued to the floor.

Gabriel's jaw twitches, and my heart breaks for him. For years and years, he kept this secret out of respect for the woman he loved. It must have killed him when she died, but he did what he thought was best for Lena. It's clear to everyone around that he never expected her to learn of her true parentage in such a traumatic way—if ever.

"I love this place. I know I've been whining about getting out, but I always figured one day I'd raise my pups here," she adds, tears cracking her armor. She furiously wipes them from her cheeks. "I don't know why Mom never told me..."

"She wanted to wait. Until you were older," Gabriel says softly.

Lena scratches at a loose thread in the table runner. "I'm furious with her. Do you know how it feels? To be mad at your dead mother? It *sucks*."

Sam and Dom quietly rise to their feet.

Lena's gaze freezes them in place. "Don't go. This isn't some Hallmark movie heart-to-heart. It's just facts. I'm saying I stayed for the pack. That's all."

"Lena, you'll always be welcomed here. Even if you'd gone..." Gabriel trails off.

"No. I don't want to be treated differently because I'm your—because you feel guilty. I've been accepted to a bunch of colleges, and I'm turning 20 in a week, so I'll start this semester. I can run on the weekends and on the full moon." She explains her plan very methodically like she practiced it a lot. "Classes start in three weeks."

I figure Jeff was supposed to be at the other end of this speech.

"I have the money. I'll go home now and get things in order at the house," she says.

Gabriel scratches the back of his neck. "Is it really what you want?"

She meets his gaze head-on. "Yes." There's a hint of defiance in the word like she expects him to fight her on this. Like she prepared a rebuttal for whatever he's going to say.

"Can I help you pack... or something?" Gabe asks awkwardly.

"No." She bites her lip, and her arms fall at her sides. "Not today. Maybe tomorrow."

"Tomorrow." Gabriel's gaze follows her until the door closes behind her, and I swear we all exhale at the same time.

"She's been thinking about this for a while. It's not about you," I assure him.

"Hmph." He turns on his heels and walks off to the bathroom.

I was hoping for a change in our dynamic, but the crazy-hot, sinful sex we had yesterday doesn't seem to have affected him one bit. He's not inclined to spill his feelings to me.

Last night was a game changer. I'd convinced myself over the years that my ex-husband, Ludovic, was the antithesis of what I actually wanted. That the controlling, jealous and powerful man was the embodiment of all that I hated. Gabriel's touch reminded me why I stayed so long, why I was lured to him in the first place.

It sickens me to draw similarities between them, but here it is.

Both giving orders.

Both responsible for their people's well being.

Both grasping at straws to uphold traditions.

But their core is what sets them apart. Where Ludovic rules by fear and manipulation, Gabriel earns the respect of his men. They chose him, not because he has royal blood, but because he's a fierce and just leader.

He's commanding in life and in bed.

Doesn't mean he's perfect, but he's bewitching, and I wish I had more time...

Sam cooks a delicious steak dinner.

There's wine, chocolate mousse, followed by more wine.

We laugh and play Scrabble.

Gabriel growls whenever Sam uses a medical term.

Dom peeks into the bag when he draws tiles, but none of us call him out on it.

It's so fun and easy, no wonder the guys prefer living together. Their banter is hilarious.

"Where did you live before?" I ask, scoring 42 points for DAZE on a triple word square.

Dom raises a brow. "Why?"

"This house is brand new. I'm curious." I lean over Sam to get a few chips from the bowl, and a wide grin spreads on my face. Gabriel glimpsed at my ass back there.

Our gazes meet, and he clicks his tongue, his eyes returning to his tiles.

"Dom? Will you do the honors?" Sam lays down the word HYDRANTS, earning 64 points and a small "fuck you" from every one of us.

Dom clears his throat. "We lived here before, in the old house."

"The old house you..." Gabe trails off, the corner of his mouth quirking.

"I burned down the old house," Dom mumbles unhappily.

My eyes widen. "What? Seriously?"

"He had a sudden urge to run and left a stack of newspaper right next to the fire," Gabe explains.

"Nobody was hurt," Dom says.

Gabe glowers. "Except my centennial house that I'd build by hand."

Dom blushes, a sight both rare and cute as hell. "We built this one by hand."

"*By hand* no longer holds the same meaning as it used to. We didn't have cranes and nail guns back then."

Sam nods emphatically at that.

The teasing relents around midnight.

Sam reaches for his book and sinks deeper into the couch.

"Read it aloud," I ask him, resting my head against his thigh.

Gabriel peels himself from his chair. "That's it. I'm going to bed."

Sam's steady voice lulls me to sleep, his hand combing through my hair as Dominic massages my feet.

How would it work if I didn't have to go? Would it be this perfect? My heart bleeds at the obvious answer. Yes. If I'd met them with a clean slate, I could have been happy.

The truth is: I don't want to leave. Not in a few days, not in a week. Not ever.

I love my wolves.

SEA OF LOVERS

VICKY

"*B*abe, I really have to go," Dom peels me off him.

A big pout settles on my mouth. "What's this suddenly urgent errand about, anyway?"

"I didn't ask."

"But Sam is spending the night with the recruits."

"You fed last night." He pecks me on the lips.

I stick out my tongue, resenting his accurate math. Sam and Dom have been all work and no play ever since Scrabble night. Gabriel has kept them so busy that I've barely got a taste of them.

The guilt ramps up by the day, and I know I'm sticking around longer than I should, but I'm unable to make up my mind about how to say goodbye. It nearly tore me apart to sneak out last time, and I don't want them to hate me after I'm gone.

I find myself questioning everything.

Truth is, suicide doesn't appeal to me at all, my martyr side is not quite developed enough for me to fall on my sword. A big part of me wants to kill as much of Ludovic's men as possible, but that's selfish. And if Gabriel knew the truth, he'd probably be the first in line to silence me forever.

The sight of the opened basement door stops my depressing train of thought. A burst of heat tingles across my belly while I climb down the stairs.

The hinges whine.

Gabriel is pacing his room like a prisoner dragging his feet along the walls of his cell. The bedside lamp is on, but other than that the room is dark and... sort of romantic? The smell of clean sheets hangs in the air, and my stomach flip-flops. The alpha kept Sam and Dom occupied on purpose, and a giddy smile threatens to show on my face.

"Took you long enough." His abs tighten, his arms flexed in a perfect picture of masculinity and impatience.

A volcanic wave washes over my skin at the clear implication of his words. "You didn't say anything."

"I sent them away, didn't I?" He closes the door behind me, the click of the bolt melting my insides.

I twist around to face him. "And that was supposed to be clear how?"

He looks me up and down, his eyes feasting on my curves until I feel a clench down there. "Strip."

I huff but unfasten my fashion belt. I've been dying for a second taste of him; I don't want him to change his mind. I pass the straps of my cotton dress over my arms, and it pools at my feet like a black wave.

Gabriel's heavy gaze follows my every move as I unclasp my bra and fling it to the side. With a wink, I slingshot my underwear at his face.

He catches the pink fabric in midair. "Touch yourself."

A wide grin on my lips, I snake my hand down my body. A thick coat of arousal spreads on my fingers, and Gabriel is entranced by the sight.

Circling me, he grips his hair and tugs at it violently like he's torn about what to do. His salt-and-seaweed scent floats toward me, making my mouth water.

Finally, he grunts and tears at his pants. "Lie down."

"Here? There's a bed right there." I point to the king-sized beauty behind him.

He grunts. "I don't want to burn my bed."

"Nobody ever comes here."

"Lie down."

Our eyes meet, our breaths shorts and shallow.

Hell if I'll be forced to do anything, but I want to lie down and see him descend on me with that deliciously dark and desperate expression on his face.

His fists ball, curl, and flex. "Christ, Blondie! Now!"

The laminate wood is cold against my back.

Gabriel towers over me and strokes himself once. Twice.

I lick my lips. I didn't get to see anything the other night. Not the intense fire burning in his eyes, not the glory of his beautiful, engorged cock, not the bunch of his muscles as he lowers himself to the ground.

The pinch of his face tells me how badly he wants it, and he squeezes my knees. "Spread your legs."

I rebel and keep my thighs shut tight. "Kiss me."

"Blondie," he growls, pulling at my knees again.

"My name is Vicky, and if you want to fuck me, you'll kiss me." I'm not budging. This is a test. Alpha sex is hot, but to borrow a page from Sam's book, I'm not a piece of meat.

His mouth crashes to mine, and I spread for him.

He pulls me onto his waiting cock in one quick, frenzied motion. A low howl rumbles at the back of his throat, and we sink into the kiss, our mouths gliding in sync with his thrusts. I dig my nails in his shoulders. He's not as defensive as before, allowing my thrall to spur him on.

It's urgent and delirious, our bodies sliding against one another, our skin singing at the friction, our hands grabbing and scratching for something to hold on to.

With no warning, he pulls out and jumps to his feet. I whimper from the loss before he plucks me from the floor and carries me to the bed. He hooks one leg on his shoulder, and I wrap the other around his waist. This angle allows him to slide even deeper. I bit my lips, my arms spread over my head, my hands grasping at the sheets.

"Tell me which you prefer."

I press my lips together not to smile and ignore the question.

He bites down on my breast, his tongue swirling around my nipple. "Tell me."

"Sam's the best kisser. Dom's got an amazing spirit."

With a dark laugh, he places an open-mouthed kiss on my calf. "Not what I meant."

His energy crashes into me, and my jaw slacks in surprise, a hot pant dying on my lips. The rush is incredible. I'm full before it starts, his powers cascading and rippling inside me like a whole different kind of food. As if I've been eating spaghetti forever, and he feeds me with... hydrogen.

He groans, his eyes hooded, clearly dealing with the full force of my own powers. "Which do you prefer?"

"You. Definitely you." And I'm not embellishing. This is something else, this is life-changing, this is... "How do you do that?" I've been with plenty of demons before. Powerful ones at that. He must be doing some kind of spell for it to feel so. Fucking. Good.

He snickers. "It's my secret."

My toes curl as he hits my sweet spot again and again, my walls swelling around him, my moans and grunts egging him on. "Gabriel!"

"Scream."

And I do. I scream my release to the empty house, the pleasure melting down my soul and my bones until I'm a puddle of Gabriel-worship.

All of the sudden, he grips my hair and pulls me to the edge of the bed.

"Come here. I want to fuck your perfect, witty mouth." His fingers dig in my scalp as he guides me toward his aching cock.

I resist. "What if I don't feel like it?" I taunt, testing his limits again, but I'm already sold.

His tip bumps against my closed lips. "Then I won't go down on you later."

The word ripples across my heart. He's making plans for *later*.

I open wide for him until his hardness hits the back of my throat and squeeze the base. About a third of him doesn't fit inside my mouth. My cheeks hollowed out, I alternate licks, sucks, and scrapes, his hard hand at the back of my head. His cues are straightforward, his hips unapologetic about thrusting deep.

The normal dynamics of sex are all skewed with Gabriel. With any other man, this part would feel like I'm offering him a treat, but somehow, the alpha makes it seems like he's doing *me* a favor. He's making himself physically vulnerable, which shows trust. And it's hot as hell.

I hum when his balls tighten.

Hot jets of cum fill my mouth, and I swallow them hungrily.

"Fuck, you're too good at that." He breathes before crashing to his back on the bed.

I mold my body to his side, and he starts playing with my hair. Each gentle tug is pulling at my heart strings.

We stay like that for the longest time, not talking.

When the rumble of the freezer coaxes me out of my post-bliss phase, I ask, "Do you think Lena will be okay?"

"Yes. She's a strong, independent woman."

I tuck my arm under my head and look at my lover. "Would you have told her?"

"Maybe. I don't know. Her mother always said we'd tell her when she turned eighteen, but back then we still had a decade to think about it. And after she died, it seemed wrong to strip Lena of another parent."

"You did right by her, Gabriel. Jeff's jealousy is to blame for what happened, not you. If he'd truly wanted the best for Lena, he wouldn't have started a war in her name."

He combs his hair away from his forehead. "I know."

My gaze falls to his nautical star tattoo. "Where are you from?"

"I was a Catalan sailor before I was bitten."

I always assumed Gabriel was a born wolf. I don't know why.

"What happened?" I lick my way up his torso, tracing the shape of his tattoo like I want to drink the ink, and he lets me.

"What happened too often back then. A wolf stuck on a boat goes wild, and the rest is history."

I rap my fingers against his abs, a thin film of sweat highlighting each ridge. "You didn't choose this life."

"It chose me, but I've never had any regrets." He braces his arm behind his head and stares at the ceiling. "I'm jealous of them. You know why? They can stroll around town smelling like you and nobody really gives a shit. Whereas I have to play games. I hate games. And I hate you for being so damn beautiful that I play them anyway."

I straddle him. "Then stop playing. Fuck me up there and tell everyone else to mind their own business."

He tenses below me, his face unreadable.

Grinning, I slowly rub the length of my body against his chest. "Or not. But if you have to burn your bed, we might as well make it count."

He presses on the small of my back, pulling me closer until I'm flush against him. "You're not wrong."

I giggle as he flips us over and claims my lips, pressing me down into the mattress.

"What's this?" His thumb grazes my tattoo.

A tight knot forms in my throat. "A splatter seemed like the right way to cover up the mistake underneath."

"Why didn't you have it removed?"

"I didn't want to forget, but I needed to move on."

His mesmerizing gaze holds me captive, and the kiss that follows is strangely gentle. "I'm going to ravage you with my mouth."

"Gabriel!" Dom's roar echoes on the walls, and there's no doubt that something is wrong. We both tense and look at the ceiling.

The door bursts open.

"Gabriel!" he stops cold at the sight of us. In slow motion, his shocked face morphs into a knowing grin. Dominic lowers his voice to resemble Gabriel's. "No, Dom, you're wrong. I don't like her that way at all. She's annoying, and there's a thousand girls I'd fuck before her. I don't understand the appeal, really."

I smack my lover on the arm. "You said that?"

Gabe throws Dominic an unimpressed glance. "I might have said that."

"Oh... you're full of shit."

Dom grins from ear to ear.

"What's the emergency?" Gabe asks.

"Vicky's missing."

Gabriel flips him off.

Dom sobers up. "No, seriously. There's a horde of vampires at the west border."

WASTED TIME

VICKY

"There were about 30 of them. The scent was nauseating. Like inhaling smoke," Dom explains.

All the bliss and happiness drain out of me and leaves a quivering mess in its place. That's impossible. Alec didn't go to France and back so quickly. These things take time. Unless the bastard lied to me the other day, and the cavalry was already in place.

Dom motions to his upper arm. "This tall guy showed me his tattoo. A cross and a rose. He said his king wanted to talk to my leader tonight at dusk."

My heart sinks. Ludovic Delacroix hasn't left his magic lands in decades. I'd be flattered if I wasn't so terrified.

"Are you telling me Ludovic Delacroix is on my doorstep with his people?" Gabriel's voice is hollow, and he yanks his jeans up.

Dom wrinkles his nose. "Who?"

Sam appears at the bottom of the stairs. "The vampire king of Europe. He's got an army—an actual army."

Gabriel transforms into a war general. His back is straight, his face blank. The weight of his gaze slides down my front to my hipbone. "You belong to a Delacroix, don't you?"

Sam's eyes screw shut. "Her tattoo... I never connected the dots."

My heart sinks past my feet, straight into rock-bottom. To hear Gabriel, talk about me as if I'm a *thing*, a possession, makes me sick. "I don't belong to *anyone*."

"Is Vicky even your real name?" Gabriel barks.

I shake my head no, my throat too tight for me to speak.

"And you expect us to believe you're not here on your king's orders?" Gabe says with a wicked, cynical smile.

My voice breaks enough for a torrent of tears to swell into the cracks, but my eyes are dry. "Ludovic would never have let you touch me."

The blood drains from Gabriel's face. "I heard the stories—he married a blonde-haired beauty that brought his enemies to their knees... You're Eleanor Delacroix."

The wretched name makes my heart thump hard.

"AREN'T YOU?"

"I used to be," I squeak.

Dom is still lost. "Who's Eleanor Delacroix?"

"The damn queen!" Gabe tears at his hair. "She's his fucking queen! Vampire royalty in *my* town. In my *bed*. This is worse than the serpent in the garden, this is a nuke in fucking paradise." He snatches my dress from the floor and hurls it at me. "Do you have any idea how much danger you brought on my doorstep? How many of my people could die? But you don't care! What—you got bored with your court and decided to fuck a bunch of werewolves to piss off your husband? Or were you gathering information, looking to strike against us?"

Sam gasps. "You're married?"

I press my fingers to my closed lids and breathe in deep. "We'll all scrub our skins until we're sure that I don't smell like you or you like me, and you'll take me to him. Nobody has to die."

"Going to have a little talk with your hubby?" Gabe snickers.

"Yes."

"Fine." Gabriel tears his pants off and stomps to his shower.

Sam stays glued to his spot. I rush past him, and the starkness in his eyes rips me in two.

Dom follows me upstairs. "What are you going to do?"

"I'm going to surrender."

He grabs my arm and pulls me toward him. "Like hell! Talk to me! I don't care about a stupid name. I know you."

The unconditional affection pouring out of him chokes me. He steps into the shower with me, and I cower into his heat.

"Tell me the truth. I can handle it," he says, tracing soothing circles on my back.

My story pours out of me like the water raining from the shower head. "I was sixteen when I met him. He didn't know what I was. Hell, I didn't know what I was. My mother had died when I was six. But as I grew, men began to take notice. After the men came the beasts. I was abducted and sold to a supernatural auction house. A beautiful virgin with a weird magical signature can make you a pretty penny there. Ludovic was waiting to buy some necklace when they wrenched me onto the stage."

Dom squeezes my hand.

"Our eyes met across the room. I can still remember the thrill in my bones. Despite everything, he was a gorgeous beast. He bought me and killed my kidnappers as I cheered." The memory tastes like blood on my lips. "He was set on marrying me, but his advisers huffed. He was to be wed to a proper vampire princess, not some human girl from the streets, so he decided to turn me into a vampire and fed me his blood. I was awakened as a vandella by the dark king of Europe's oldest and most dangerous vampire clan. When he realized what I truly was, after I changed into what I am now, he married me in a fortnight."

"So... you loved him," Dom trails off awkwardly.

"I admired his power and charisma. I had nothing; he had

everything. Every female wanted him, and yet he preferred me. The change awakened a part of me I couldn't fathom. Couldn't control. I got lost in it for a while. I was to be worshiped by the most powerful beast on Earth. Loved." I snicker, but the sound is hollow. "Only he never loved me. He loved to own me. Loved to parade me around and make the other princes jealous. Loved to threaten to cut off their heads when they looked at me for too long."

Dom kisses my hands. "He was jealous?"

"Madly jealous. As my powers grew, many tried to have me. They all failed. A few died trying. It drove Ludovic crazy, and he became even more violent and controlling. I was living in a hell of my own making. You do not leave a man like Ludovic Delacroix. You serve him or you die. Until Etienne. Etienne Delacroix was Ludovic's oldest cousin. He was a kind man, and he recognized my situation for what it was: hopeless.

"He came to me in the dead of night, and I thought he was another horny vampire willing to risk his life to get a taste of his queen. But he offered me something better. Freedom. He helped me fake my death. After my funeral, he switched the body in the coffin and brought me to America where he woke me up from the near-death state. I'd lost a month of my life, but I was free."

"But you've been running ever since," Dominic sums up.

"I knew he'd find me one day. I've made my peace with it."

Dominic's hands are shaking. "Fuck peace. Fuck him. Let me talk to them. Sam is only upset because of the marriage thing, and Gabe... I'll make it work; I promise."

I nod and watch him leave.

Numb, I pat myself dry, grab clothes fresh out of the dryer, and slip out through the window, knowing there is no other way. If I stay and fight, dozens will die. At least, this way, I know my wolves will survive.

I steal the Jeep and drive straight to the West border, a roadblock of cars and soldiers waiting for me next to the fields of barley.

The Delacroix's black flag contrasts against the pinkish sky, and I draw in a deep breath.

I had a good ten years. It counts for something.

But I underestimated Dominic's stubbornness. My three wolves catch up, Gabriel's truck roaring behind me.

I warn them off with my hands, begging them silently not to come out. The last thing I need is for three men to escort me to my psycho husband... If he gets an inkling of how I truly feel, he'll kill them.

The devil's silhouette clashes against the light behind him, and the sun falls under the horizon at this exact moment, like Ludovic is stepping out of some hellish dimension. The shape of his proud jaw and angular cheekbones feel so familiar, it knocks the wind out of me. Very few vampires have blue eyes, and he looks like an angel.

I know better.

There is no beauty here.

All I see when I look at him is the face of who I was when we were together. A lost girl with an empty life and an emptier heart. The thought of her makes me ill, and my legs are begging me to run.

Looking at him is like staring into a black mirror, my flaws magnified by his presence.

My soul trembles as our eyes meet, the ghost of who I was rattling in my chest. I stand up straight, knowing how furious he gets when I slouch. I loved him once, though this particular nugget of my past is blurry and out of reach.

Shock and fury flicker on his face, but the emotions are quickly eclipsed by the crafted mask of a king.

I used to believe that love had to be jealous and painful. All because of this man. This demon. This monster.

He offers me his hand. "Come with me now, *mon amour*, and I'll let them live."

I plaster a sexy smile on my face and strut to him with a forced spring in my step. I don't spare one glance to the men I love.

I can imagine Sam's eyes dimming and the angry frown on Dom's face as I plant a voluptuous kiss on Ludovic's mouth. My heart hammers against my ribs, each beat more painful than the last, and I feel like I might shatter. I don't look at my wolves. I don't say goodbye.

Instead, I bat my eyelashes and graze my husband's stomach, the tips of my fingers pulsating with fear, but my eyes are all sugar and sex.

Ludovic loves sugar and sex. That's why he chose me.

"Who cares about them? Bring me home."

SHADOWS

DOMINIC

"Why are you packing?" Gabriel asks.

Gripping a pair of underwear with one hand and a Smith and Wesson in the other, I give Gabe the stink eye. "We're going after her."

"No."

My wolf shivers at the stern command, but I rebel. "What do you mean, no?"

"She made her choice and left. It's settled." He presses his lips together and looks out the window.

I pace my room, cramming a pair of jeans and iron rounds into my duffel bag. "Nothing is settled. She left because her crazy ex-husband was threatening to kill us all."

"Do you hear yourself? How naïve you sound? He's not her ex-husband. He's her very-much-current husband, and she left with him."

I roll my eyes at his total asshole-ness. "And you didn't smell the overwhelming fear rolling off her when she laid eyes on him?"

His jaw ticks.

I point a finger at his face. "We're going after her."

"I can't let you do that."

"Let me?" My fists curl. If he insists on being the most ridiculous hypocrite on the planet, I'll have to punch him.

"Be reasonable, kid, and realize what you're asking. I can't compromise the whole town to make your dick happy."

My eyes bulge. "You are such an asshole, I can't even—" He's so stiff that he's almost shaking, and I wave to his I'm-about-to-explode body language. "You see it, right? This ain't about saving the town. This is about your trust issues with women. You're angry with her for lying to you."

He snarls, his hand slicing through the space between us. "Don't go there."

"Oh, I will gladly go there, boss. Someone ought to give it to you straight. Let's recap: alpha marries a fellow wolf to appease the community, but only gives her scraps because he's in love with a married, mated woman. Said alpha gets betrayed by his wife, giving him the excuse to treat all women like shit. How am I doing so far?"

"Calm down, kid. We can talk tomorrow when you're done being a dickhead." He walks away like I'm the one acting immaturely. Like I'm a fucking toddler throwing a tantrum.

My blood boils. "I'm not going to be here tomorrow."

"If you pursue those vampires, you'll be doing so without the support of the pack."

"The pack. Right. Because the pack is always so supportive." Ten years living together, hunting together, breathing together, and he still gives me this pack shit. Yes, he's our alpha. Yes, he's responsible for a lot of us. But Sam and I aren't just a part of his pack. We're fucking family.

"She was only using us."

I pass a hand over my face and look over to Sam for support. His face is still green, and if Gabriel is about to blow, Sam looks ready to faint. "Sam? A little help here?"

Gabriel throws his hands up in the air. "Nobody is going after her. That's an order."

A lump forms in my throat, and I know I'm going to regret my next words, but I can't help it. I throw my bag over my shoulder and barrel out the door. "See you in hell, boss."

JUST LIKE A PILL

VICKY

I'm chained up on a fancy bed in some New York penthouse. The night lights of the skyscrapers keep me company. I've been here for five days, restless and wanton.

The silk fabric of my wedding gown is wrapped around me like a white shroud.

The maid comes in to clean me, scrubbing my skin with a sponge. Ludovic has sent her in ten times already, but he still insists that I reek of wolf.

He wants me to beg, and so far, I haven't been inclined. I'm fading fast. If I don't have sex with him soon, I'll die.

I'm almost fine with it.

We're going in circles, having the same conversation day after day, hour after hour.

"Why did you leave me?" he asks again after the maid leaves. He's delusional enough to believe I used to be happy with him.

I tried a dozen answers. None of them stuck, so I try another. "I got bored."

"Tell me the truth, *mon amour*."

I can't tell him that I woke up one day and realized he'd become a nasty, cruel man. One I simply couldn't love. Or maybe I can't admit that he's always been that man, but I was too damaged and desperate to see him for what he was, instead of what I wished him to be.

His hand grazes the inside of my thigh, and I bite my lips at the hunger spiraling up my spine.

I hate him, and I hate myself for even thinking about doing this, but I need it. I need it bad. And Ludovic knows me, knows how to work my treacherous body so it's ripe for the picking.

But I won't relent. Not this time.

He laces up my wedding dress, the tight corset knocking the wind out of me. "It drives me mad thinking how many men had you. That these disgusting wolves touched you..."

I force my breathing to stay even. "Why are we still talking about the wolves?"

"They let you go..."

"Why wouldn't they?" I rest my head on the pillow, playing it cool. He's obsessed with them, and I'm terrified that he'll change his mind and hunt them down.

"Maybe I'm crazy, but I had a feeling they might be attached to you. And you to them." This is a test. He's still suspicious. "Do you think they've forgotten all about you?"

"Yes." I say the word, but my voice cracks, and Ludovic flattens me to the bed, his hand pushing my head into the mattress until I can hardly breathe.

"I knew it! I knew you liked them."

"They are nothing," I insist.

He snaps my chains out of the posters and flips me to my back. "Liar! You lied and went back on your vows. You were supposed to be mine *jusqu'à ce que la mort nous sépare, chérie*."

I spit at his feet. "You're mean and violent and everyone in your court hates you. I left because I couldn't stand to spend another day in your suffocating presence."

"You'll pay for that." He yanks me into the other room by the chains.

I struggle to stay upright, my bare feet slipping against the cool tiles. I tumble and fall to my ass, the skirt of my dress absorbing most of the impact.

"Look what I found on the roof last night," Ludovic says, his tone perversely giddy.

Dominic. Sam. They are tied to the wall behind them by their wrists and ankles, and they both look rough. Beaten. Blue and purple bruises deform their angry faces.

I press a hand to my mouth not to vomit.

"Now, I'm going to expose you for the whore that you are. I know how hungry you get. In a few hours, you won't hate me so much. You'll beg for my cock, and they'll watch me fuck you. They'll watch me fuck you until you're screaming, and then you can choose which one dies first."

A single tear slides down my cheek. "Let's make a deal."

"Too late for that."

My head hurts, my rebellious heart pooling at my feet. "Don't you want your perfect Eleanore back? Your dutiful queen. You kill them; you can keep me here and fuck me, but I'll never be yours again. What will the others say? They know I'm alive. How badly will it reflect on you if I'm not seen at court, holding your hand, doing *your* bidding, sucking *your* cock?"

I cringe and screw my eyes shut. Ludovic is hanging to my every word. "Let them go, and I'll be by your side *forever*."

He grabs my hair and plants a desperate kiss on my lips. I reciprocate. This monster is my monster, for better or worse.

"You go back on your deal and they die. Them and all the dirty wolves living in that boring little town," he says quietly.

I incline my head. "I understand."

He breaks the chains and arches a brow. "They'll still have to watch me fuck you."

I'm shaking, but I can't let it show. I've got to prove I can honor my end of this nasty contract.

And so I kiss him, digging my nails into his scalp until it hurts. This is my last chance. If I mess up again, he'll kill them and keep me as a slave. His body is familiar, and I go to this place in my mind where the only two things that matter are hunger and lust. I've had to retreat there many times when I didn't feel like having sex but had to.

I keep my eyes open, but secretly, I'm thousands of miles away in the cabin, nestled in Sam's embrace as he reads, his brow bent in concentration. Dom plops down next to us and massages my feet, teasing me for being so cold-blooded. Sam casts his book aside and caresses the nape of my neck.

In my head, I'm surrounded by my wolves, not here, about to spread my legs for my monstrous husband. Not about to scream his name in pleasure so he spares them, an act that will no doubt smear their memories of me forever.

And forever is going to be a long, long time.

NUMB

VICKY

*E*urope is beautiful in the fall.

My soul is a fallen leaf withering in the lush Delacroix gardens.

I bow my head and kneel at Ludovic's feet in front of the whole court, begging for my king's forgiveness. I offer him my life for my rebellion. He extends his hand and pulls me to my feet, gracing me with his mercy.

Vicky is dead. Eleanor lives.

The beautiful silk gown feels like a noose tightening around my neck as I roam the halls of the castle, wondering in which corner he's hiding, waiting to surprise me with another kiss. My body belongs to him, but my heart is far away, lying on a tartan blanket, looking up at American stars.

I plaster a smile on my face because I know what will happen if I don't. I slip back into my old ways.

Days at court feels like months. Nights in Ludovic's bed blur into one another. He's ravenous, making up for lost time. And the worst part is, a buried part of me stirs to life in his presence. A black, cruel part. It whispers that I deserve no better.

I chose him.

I drank from him.

I spoke a vow.

I wore a white dress and sealed my fate with a kiss.

The stars flicker until there's nothing but darkness. My heart shrivels to a stump, useless and bothersome, a reminder of what I lost.

I'm dead inside, but Ludovic will be deader when I'm done with him.

They'll eviscerate me for it and feed me to their hounds, but I'm going to do it.

I'm going to kill my husband.

HUMAN

VICKY

*I*t takes time to get what I need without arousing suspicion. A candle. Aconite. Sugar.

A knife.

The candle wax mixes with the aconite and sugar, and I use it to coat the blade. The sugar masks the scent.

When it's finally time to do it, my palms aren't sweaty. My hands do no shake. My eyes do not give me away. I wait for him to be on the crest of his dirty pleasure, my legs spread on each side of his waist and my body numb before I slit his throat. It's calm. Messy.

It works because he does not expect it. Despite my betrayal, he struggles to see me as anything other than the sixteen-year-old girl he rescued from the streets. He missed the ten years that hardened me. The aftermath of his cruelty that sharpened my senses and sculpted my muscles.

Disbelief paints his face. In his last seconds, he can't wrap his royal brain around the fact that I killed him. Me. His once dutiful wife.

A dark burgundy wave washes over me when I finish the job and behead him in one terrible movement. His body explodes into dust, and I stagger to the mattress, gathering a film of particles on my hands and watching them fall with quiet wonderment.

It's incredible that a man who held so much power over me, a vampire who ruled over a fucking continent, a creature that cramped my stomach with so much fear, can be flesh one second and ashes the next.

Drenched in his blood, I wrap a white robe around my frame and tear off the white silk garter belt he forced me to wear. I won't try to escape. What's the point? I'll face my punishment with glee, knowing I erased a monster from the world. An immortal one at that.

I count the minutes until the guards come to look for him and console myself by thinking the crown will go to his much gentler brother.

The door opens, and I hold my breath. I expected the guards. Or my servant. Anything but this.

Confused, I pinch myself to make sure I'm not already dead, but Gabriel is here, in Ludovic's bedchamber, armed to the teeth.

Adrenaline rushes through me for the first time in weeks. My palms are drenched in sweat. My hands shake. My eyes water. "Are you fucking kidding me?"

That's clearly not the welcome he expected. His eyes are wild. He takes in the carnage and tucks his gun at his back.

It's really him. His salty but masculine scent lingers in the air like an ocean breeze. "What are you doing here?"

The belt of grenades wrapped around him falls to the ground with a faint *clack*. "I'm here to rescue you."

A chuckle bubbles up my throat, and I press my hand to my mouth.

He hugs me, pressing me to his chest like I'm his anchor to the world. "I thought you were dead."

"Why did you come?" My voice is nothing but a bitter rasp. I choke on a sob, and my knees give out from under me. "You should leave before they find you."

He holds me up, his body heat dizzying. "Those bastards will never hurt you again. You're coming with me."

Freedom. It's too good to be true.

I'm not moving a muscle, and he frowns. When his warm hands clamp my fingers, I stare into his stormy gray eyes. "Are Sam and Dominic okay?"

He grazes my cheek. "They're fine. They're waiting for us. So we can bring you home."

"Home..."

"Yes."

"But you hate me."

He doesn't say another word. Instead, he grips my arm, yanks me to my feet and crushes his lips to mine. It's a violent kiss, one that takes all and gives nothing back. My jaw hurts from the force of it while my heart beats harder for every brush.

His hands tremble, and he pulls back. "You're one hell of a woman. I can't believe I let this beast take you away." The next kiss is tender, apologetic. "I'll make it up to you, Vicky."

He's never used my name before. It sounds different on his lips.

It sounds true.

My fingers clench around his. "They'll get revenge for this."

He kisses my forehead. "They can try."

He twines our fingers and pulls me along the stone corridors. The servants' staircase takes us to the kitchens, an area I've never visited, but Gabriel seems to know the way. We reach a more modern section and erupt into a stone-covered area full of cars.

My eyes meet Dom's. The wolf is sitting in a van, ready to race off. His hazel depths are both sad and warm.

"Hands in the air!" Alec's voice stops both Gabriel and I cold. The click of a gun resonates in the interior garage.

We're inches from the catering van he and Dom probably used to get into the castle. Sweat drips along my neck.

We were so close.

"He's dead?" Alec asks, his voice dry and dangerous.

I spin around to face him. "Deader than dead. Dusted. It's over."

Alec nods slowly and lowers his gun. "Go on, then. I'll give you a head start."

My breath catches. "What?"

"Take care, Elle."

Gabriel opens the back of the van and pulls me along with him.

Dom drives out of the gates, and my heart is flying out of my chest. The world blurs beyond the windows. I cry my heart out, my entire body shaking in Gabe's arms.

When we park next to a private plane, my hiccups subside. Gabe gently peels me off him and the doors open wide.

Sam leads me to the plane. I think we take off moments after the door closes behind us.

There's a couch in the back. Sam kisses my forehead and holds me to his chest. His heartbeat is as delirious as mine.

Dom is about to slump next to us when Gabriel stops him. "Give them a moment. Sam is exactly what she needs right now."

He's right, and the ice in my blood finally thaws.

Sam wraps his arms around my shoulders. "We shouldn't have let you leave with him. I'm so sorry."

"You came back for me. Twice." If he hadn't let me go, this story would have ended in a bloodbath, and we wouldn't have won. Bad things happen for good reasons. I'm okay with how things turned out.

From Alec's reaction to Ludovic's death, I figure no one will mourn him for long.

"It took us forever to find you," Sam says in a breathless whisper. The heat of his regret tingles across my face.

"I killed him. Ludovic."

He holds his breath.

I twine our fingers, my sight riveted on them. I thought I'd never see those healing hands again. "Does it bother you? That I could kill my own husband?"

He tucks a strand of hair behind my ear. "From what Dom told me, he was more of a master than a husband. He wasn't good to you."

"I wasn't good then, either."

"The past doesn't matter." He brings my hand to his mouth and kisses it. "I don't care who you were before. What you were called or who you slept with. I want *you*, Vicky. A chance to be by your side. To be your future."

"I want that too." To be whole. Unbroken. It always seemed like a fantasy, but a spark of hope burns bright in my chest where the gaping hole used to be. I tried to manage on my own. For ten years, I made sure not to rely on anyone. I refused to form lasting attachments. I lived a half-dead life.

The rumble of the wheels makes the floor shake as we accelerate down the runway. The plane lifts into the air. I feel like I might rise into the clouds myself.

As improbable as it sounds, we're going *home*.

I'M NOT DEAD

VICKY

*W*e make it back to the cabin. Our cabin. It feels like cheating to call it that, but it's true. When I was young, I bounced from foster family to foster family. When Ludovic bought me, I moved in with him and spent the ten years after that on the run. I've never had a home. But this *feels* like home.

The sum of the rush of adrenaline, the jet lag, and the emotional trauma liquefies my brain, and I sleep for what seems like a month, though it's probably closer to a few days. When I come to, Sam draws me a bath in Gabriel's bathroom.

The Jacuzzi is bigger than the one upstairs, and my lips quirk at the knowledge that Gabriel takes baths by himself. I sense an endless string of teasing coming.

After washing the dirt and dread from my skin, I look at my reflection. The bruises from the last few weeks are almost gone, and the woman in the mirror has never looked stronger. I faced my demons and exorcised them from this Earth.

My pale purple irises are pulsing with hunger, and for the first time since my abduction, I welcome it. The self-hatred I nurtured for a decade exploded into dust at the same time as Ludovic, and I left all my baggage in his cold castle.

I'm ready to move on. To a home. To a life. To a love.

Or several...

I'm done running.

After braiding my hair, I join my wolves in the alpha's room. They are all standing, waiting for me.

A breakfast tray in his hands, Dom motions to Gabriel's bed.

The alpha's gaze falls to the faded purple marks on my legs, and his jaw clenches. "I should have killed them all. I should have set that damn castle on fire."

I pour maple syrup on the thin, steamy crêpe. Dom really outdid himself. "Ludovic's men aren't to blame for what he did, just as Xavier's weren't."

"I should have torn his heart out of his chest."

"You were upset." I fork a piece into my mouth. Yum.

Gabe paces the room, his fists balled at his sides. "Stop finding excuses for me, it drives me nuts. Scream at me. Curse my name. Anything but this."

"It kills you that I'm reasonable?" I raise a brow.

"It kills me that Dom was right," Gabriel grunts.

I deposit the empty tray on the desk. As good as it was, it's not nearly enough. I walk to Gabriel and crush my mouth to his. He tenses but allows it. His thumbs caress my jawline, and I glance back to Sam and Dom.

Sam's blue eyes search mine. "You need to feed."

"Yes," I admit. I've been starving for their touch ever since I was last here.

Dom cracks a smile. "We've been arguing over who gets to be with you first."

"So we thought..." Gabe trails off, caressing the ridge of my shoulder blade.

My gut melts into liquid fire. To say that this is my wildest fantasy would be selling this moment short.

Sam takes my hand into his and kisses my wrist. "But you get to choose."

I feel like a goddess, my mortal lovers awaiting my orders, and it's mighty hot. Even Gabriel looks ready to submit to my decision despite the lust burning on his proud face.

I can't choose between them. Not now, not ever. And the best part is, I don't have to.

Dom unfastens the sash holding my robe in place, and I gasp as Gabriel's large hands pry it off my shoulders. The silk bunches at my feet, goosebumps running wild all over my skin.

Sam's hand travels up my leg. "We talked about it."

"And we want you to stay." Dom cups my breast, his fingers caressing the underside, and I arch into him.

"Permanently." Sam places a kiss on the tender flesh of my inner thigh.

Gabriel presses me against his hard chest. "You need us."

"And we need you." Dom licks my pulse point.

Sam slides two fingers inside me. It's too much sensation, and my eyes roll inward. I rest my head on Gabe's shoulder and snake a hand around Dom's neck. My legs are pure jelly because of what Sam is doing down there, but Gabe grips my waist.

"Okay. I'll stay." I breathe, distracted.

Gabe pinches my ass. "She said *okay*."

Dom grazes my nipple with his thumb. "We need more than *okay*."

Sam sucks my clit into his mouth.

"Yes! Yes! Yes! God!"

Gabriel grins against my cheek. "That's better."

He sinks two fingers inside me from behind while Sam's tongue plays hide-and-seek with my throbbing flesh.

The three of them... it's all so new and overwhelming. Maybe I should want to take things slow. Maybe I shouldn't feel so free, but their voices are rich with promises, and their offer is empowering. They are *asking*, not taking.

There's so much desire clogging the air, three hungry tongues, so many hands... I can't keep track. I only know how it feels. Like heaven and hell wrapped into one sweet, heady dream.

Dom and Gabriel hold me steady as I come against Sam's mouth, the sensitive skin quivering, my insides screaming for more.

I pull the doctor to his feet and wrap my fingers around the waist of his jeans. His hand closes around my wrist like he means to stop me.

Gabriel chuckles. "Don't back out now, Sammy. Strip, lie down, and feel how much she needs you."

Sam still looks unsure and wide-eyed as he stumbles out of his clothes, but he does lie down on the bed.

Gabe and Dom fling me over the third wolf, the hot planes of his chest wonderful beneath my fingers. Sam swallows hard. I rub myself on his hardness, desperate to feel him inside me.

Dom hands me a scarf and winks. I wrap it around Sam's head to cover his eyes and lean to whisper in his ear. "Don't think. Just feel."

His hands fly to my waist, and he bites his lips, angling me right. The fire only burns brighter as I take every inch of him, my lips parted from the pleasure of finally being filled.

Dom leans against the wall and watches, his eyes brimming with desire.

I reach out with my hands. "Come closer."

He grins and shakes his head no.

Gabriel's chest glides against my back. The scrape of his teeth over my pulse point makes me gasp, and he runs his big hands up and down my front, my breasts heavier and fuller with each migration. I stretch to grip his hair.

My walls are squeezed tightly around Sam's cock, but my release is still out of reach, chased away by the promise of the headiest pleasure I've ever felt.

I sink my nails in Gabe's arm. "I need... more."

"I thought you'd never ask." His fingers drag my wetness up the path to my ass. The tip pushes against my backside, and I force my muscles to relax.

It's a tight fit.

Sam cups my ass, holding me at just the right angle as he and Gabe take turns fucking me. The thought that I have them both inside me at the same time leaves me gasping. It stretches me out in the most delicious way, such great care taken not to hurt me.

"Fuck, this is too hot." Dom grunts. He's not grinning anymore, his chest heaving with ragged breaths.

I hook my finger and motion for him to come closer.

He drags down his zipper, his cock springing to attention. A bead of precum glistens on the tip, and I lick my lips. I need to feel all three of them inside me, filling me, loving me, worshiping my body the way it was meant to be worshiped. Feeding me their love and their lust until I'm hungry again.

I come as soon as I taste his salty desire on my tongue. The pleasure is sharp and painful at first until it swells into wave after wave of pure, unadulterated bliss, each of Sam's thrusts sweeter than the last, Gabriel's tongue tracing a fiery path against my shoulder blade, every single one of Dom's tugs on my hair acting as the anchor I need not be swept by the undertow. It goes on and on and on, my wolves playing me like I'm their instrument, their gentle touch and demanding cocks writing symphonies with my body.

"Look at her. She's high with pleasure," Gabriel breathes against my neck.

And then, with perfect synchrony, they each bite down on my flesh hard enough for me to bleed. My wolves, my loves, my *mates*.

My body is shaking, but I'm still coming, my flesh hungry for them like they're the sun, the moon, the stars, and then some.

CASTLE

VICKY

I wake up, tangled in my wolves. Sam's arm hangs around my waist, and Dom's breath tickles my ear. The sheets are still damp with the remnants of our sinful, perfect night. Cocooned in their warmth, I stretch and yawn, my body lulled into a cottony laziness that threatens to spread to my limbs, but I force my eyes open. Gabriel is nowhere to be found.

I tiptoe up the staircase, the wood creaking under my foot.

The alpha is drinking coffee in the kitchen, looking out at the forest over the sink. Steam rises from his cup, and his eyes close when he takes a sip. A low rumble echoes at the back of his throat.

"It's early for coffee," I say, making my way to him. It's only five in the morning, and I'm positive Gabriel didn't get a lick of sleep.

He's naked, the curve of his ass sending electric jolts to my chest and thighs.

A sizzling warmth gleams in his gray eyes, and he sets down his mug. "A she-demon kept me awake all night."

I hook my arms around his neck, inhaling his salty, fresh scent. "You were the one who insisted on that fourth round."

"Is it bad that I want a fifth?" He raises a brow, his lips curved up in the ghost of a smile.

Our noses brush.

"How is this going to work? Do we still have to burn your bed?" I ask.

Was last night a one-time thing? It certainly didn't feel like it, but Gabe has got more to lose than all of us.

Two strong hands travel down my sides to my hips and squeeze them tight. "You're mine. Everyone will just have to get used to it."

My breath stutters, and I know better than to argue against the possessive word. "What if they don't?"

"They can find another shifter town to live in."

What happened to his strict secrecy rule? The drastic change unnerves me. "You still feel guilty." I'm grateful that he wants to make amends for his initial reaction when the skeletons of my past barreled into his town guns and swords blazing, but guilt doesn't make a very sturdy foundation on which to build... whatever this is. A foursome? Ménage? Harem?

A girl can't get this lucky, can she?

Gabe's lids flutter shut. "I'll go to my grave regretting how I treated you that day. Projecting my shit on you. I smelled the fear rolling off you. I saw the distress on your face. I saw it all, yet I was blind."

I trace his features with my fingers. His proud nose is wrinkled. His full lips are tensed. There's pain written in every crease.

Dom is carefree. Sam grieves. Gabriel is the only one who understands what it means to be broken. His trust is fragile, his heart scarred. He probably vowed to stay single forever. I know I did.

Like me, he struggles to give someone else the power to hurt him again.

A shift has taken place ever since he found me covered in Ludovic's blood. He used to hold me at arm's length. That distance between us is gone, but intimacy doesn't come naturally to him. It's a privilege. Fleeting and beautiful.

It'll probably take years before he can truly let go of the reins, if he ever does, but the fact that he wants to try is enough.

Gabriel peppers my neck with kisses, and I tilt my head back to allow him better access. My chest heaves when he brushes his bite mark, blood flooding to my center.

Gripping the back of my thighs, he picks me up, sets me down on the kitchen table, and steps between my legs. My hand travels up his defined abs.

I'll never get enough of him. His fire. His passion. It's my new drug.

He can't sleep next to me like they do.

He can't say he loves me.

But the slow, heady morning sex is filled with promises. He's making a statement by fucking me upstairs, and it's a big one. It tells me he's serious about revealing our relationship to the town. Maybe not right now, but it's on the table. Literally.

Not just that, he's freer with his kisses. I feel his plea in every brush of his tongue. *Be patient, I'll get there.*

Dom climbs up the stairs right as we finish. My legs are wrapped around Gabriel, my climax still tingling across my spine.

The impetuous shifter stops and groans, tugging at his dark hair. "Shit. The scent is just—Fuck, now I'm hard again."

I chuckle, well aware of that fact since he's not wearing underwear. Gabe rolls his eyes and nods at the young wolf with his chin up, the universal signal for *go*. I snatch Dom's wrist, pulling him along to his room. I'm so well-fed, I feel drunk.

"He fucked you upstairs," Dom says in a schoolgirl, gossipy tone.

I grin from ear to ear, giddiness crackling in my blood. "Mm-Mm."

"That's huge. Shit is going to hit the fan. This town will be talking about the three of us behind our backs for years."

"But no violence?" I chew on my bottom lip.

"I don't think so, why?"

"I'm glad. I don't want to cause more trouble."

Dom wraps his hands around my face and plants one delicious kiss on my pout. "Trouble is your middle name. It's not always going to be as easy as last night, you know. We fight. We mouth off. We're hot-blooded wolves. Sharing a mate isn't in our blood." There's playfulness in his voice, but also a real warning.

I snake my hand down his front. "You didn't complain last night."

Eyes closed, he tilts his head back and groans.

Our dynamic will need ironing out, but I'm looking forward to both the highs and lows. These men have carved their places into my heart, and angry sex is hot anyway.

Seeing them fight over me doesn't sound so bad...

Dom traces a blazing path from my shoulder to my ass with the tips of his fingers. "Plus... How are we supposed to get anything done with you running around the house naked?"

I palm his bare ass. "Said the kettle to the pot. Besides, I thought you enjoyed a challenge?"

He does a gruff woof sound and pins me to the wall, his eyes full of promises too.

FIELDS OF GOLD

VICKY

$\mathcal{T}$he wind blows through the fields of corn, the long strands waving at me in the breeze. In a few days, everything will be harvested, and the earth will be barren until spring. But while the leaves are falling and the oaks, maples, birches and willows are settling in for their winter slumber, I have never felt more awake.

My outstretched arms caress the corn stalks on both sides as I make my way to the cabin.

It's warmer than it should be for the season, the Indian summer holding strong against the threat of icy rain.

Sam catches up to me and twines our fingers. "Penny for your thoughts?"

"I know what you're doing, mister. And while I appreciate your qualifications, you're my boyfriend, not my therapist. Though if you had a therapy couch, I'd gladly make you break your code of ethics..."

"I don't have a therapist couch."

I stop and spin around. "We should get one."

Sam bumps into me because of my abrupt change of direction. I stand on the tips of my toes and crush my lips to his. His hand cups the side of my face, and he kisses me the way only Sam does, with both a quiet urgency and an unwavering patience.

"We should talk about this," he breathes.

I bury my face in his neck. "Just hold me."

"All right. I'm backing off. But you know I'm here. Night or day. I'll always be here for you if you want to talk... about whatever."

"Even types of couches?"

"Even that." With a smile, he captures my mouth again, and I walk in reverse, drinking in him until we reach the back porch.

Dominic is flipping steaks on the barbecue, the sweet richness of red meat floating through the air. He waves with his spatula and wiggles his eyebrows at my denim skirt. "How you doing?"

I trace his bare shoulder blade. "Do you cook half-naked in the winter?"

"Nope."

"Damn... I'm going to miss summer."

"Me too." He grazes the hem of my skirt. "Snow makes changing shape in the woods an unpleasant affair."

I lean into his heat and nudge his hip with mine. "Smells amazing."

He opens the barbecue lid. There are no black lines on the meat, but he stabs the first T-Bone and sets it onto a plate.

I peck him on the lips. "Cook mine a little longer."

He shakes his head. "Rare is the only way to go with a steak of this caliber."

"Your definition of 'rare' fits my description of 'raw'."

Dom grumbles. "I hope you appreciate how hard it is for me to overcook meat. If you weren't so sexy..." He steals a kiss, steak spices and beer filling my mouth. Hunger squeezes my belly.

God, if we hadn't invited Lena, I'd be tempted to start what will probably be our last dinner outside until spring with dessert...

The three of them hover around me like I'm made of a special blend of chocolate they both want to protect and devour. It's infuriatingly hot. Gabriel acts all bossy and protective, and I know he feels responsible for letting me leave in the first place. Whatever guilt he's working through won't last forever, though, so I'm milking it for all it's got.

I used my newfound influence and convinced him to join me in the bath last night. The mental image of his ridiculously sexy alpha body covered in bubbles will never leave me.

Dom spoils me with massages and overstuffed meat sandwiches.

Sam has doubled down on the kisses.

I love the attention. If it goes on any longer, I'll become the most spoiled woman on Earth.

I cut myself on a pointy splinter in the porch's railing, the wood sticking out from the tip of my index finger. "Ow." I bring the injured finger to my mouth.

The porch's door swing on its hinges as Gabe steps outside. "You're bleeding?" His hand skims the small of my back.

I huff. "It's the tiniest cut. See?"

The alpha covers my hand with his and rubs the back of it with his thumb.

"Hey, guys. Smells amazing." Lena chimes, her tall silhouette erupting from the side of the house. She's wearing red shorts and a cute black tank top, her black mane tied in a messy bun on top of her head.

Gabe sidesteps away from me, gracefully playing off the moment as though nothing happened. "Lena, hi."

"Gabriel."

The alpha joins Sam in the kitchen.

Lena wraps me up in a hug. "I'm so glad you're back."

"Me too."

"I wanted to go with them. I begged Gabriel to help," she whispers quietly.

"He told me. He also said you didn't pack for school."

"I couldn't go to college knowing you were in danger." She tucks a strand of hair behind her ear and throws me a sideways glance. "This vampire... he hurt you."

My lids flutter shut for a brief second. I know what she's working towards. I also know they all mean well. "I'm... free of him now. I'm not saying you should kill every boyfriend who's bad to you, but believe me, this vampire deserved to die. Sam is walking on eggshells, thinking I'll crack. I told him, and I'm telling you now: my ex-husband poisoned my life while he was alive. No matter how far or how fast I ran, I could feel him breathing down my neck. Now that he's dead, he has no claim over me. I get to choose to move on. And after twelve years of seeing his face in my nightmares, I've earned the right to banish him from my memories."

"That's... really brave." She wets her lips with the definite look of someone searching for something useful to say.

I chuckle and pat her back. "Hey, maybe I won't feel so brave tomorrow. That's also my prerogative." I know there might be rough patches ahead, but I am *here*. I have a life, a future. No more running, no more lies. If the Delacroix come after us, we'll fight them. Whatever drama comes our way, I have faith that my wolves have my back and I have theirs.

Lena squeezes my arm affectionately. "I'll miss you this semester."

"We can gossip about all the pretty boys who will line up to meet you over the phone."

Sam passes us both a champagne flute, and we clink our glasses together.

She reaches for my hair, and before I know it, she's tracing the scar Gabe left on my neck. "So... this thing with Gabriel. When did it start?"

"It was love at first bite," I joke.

We both snigger into our drinks.

Suddenly, a big cringe twists her mouth, and our gazes meet. "Does this make you like... my step-mother?"

My eyes bulge. "Ew! Never use that word again."

The End... for now.

WANT MORE IN THIS UNIVERSE? Read the series that started it all and glimpse into Vicky's past. **http://bit.ly/buyshadowwalker**

AUTHOR'S NOTE

Thank you for coming on this wild journey with me. Vicky was the perfect heroine to explore a steamy, fast-pace romance, and I hope you loved her story as much as I loved writing it.

If you haven't read the trilogy in which Vicky is a minor character, check it out now. It's **free** on KU.

http://bit.ly/buyshadowwalker

Or download the FREE Prequel Lost Boy here: BookHip.com/QFFVFW

I might continue with the Secrets of Wolf Creek. Lena needs to find love, too, and Gabriel won't be happy with that.

I've got another reverse harem novel and a supernatural Academy romance series in the works. To keep up with my releases and receive a bunch of exclusive extras, join my newsletter.

Click here: http://bit.ly/anyaslair

Did you know that reviews really help authors to promote their books? To support me, please review on the Amazon page.

Xoxo, Anya.

Facebook: https://www.facebook.com/AnyaJCosgrove/

SHADOW WALKER SNEAK PEEK

*R*ead the series that inspired this spin-off and see what brought Vicky to her werewolves.

Nothing stays black and white in a world full of shadows...

I'M ALANA MITCHELL, and for my twentieth birthday, I got a brand-new magical destiny instead of the laptop I was saving for.

I'm a witch. I have powers I can't control, enemies I know nothing about, and a legacy I can't begin to grasp.

There's a shadow-world out there waiting to swallow me whole, a world I didn't even know existed until I used my magic and unleashed hell upon my naïve self. From heart-eating ghouls to glamors, potions, and spells... nothing is as it seems.

A renegade demon and his brother are teaching me the ropes and driving me crazy with their I-know-better attitudes, beckoning stares and stupidly handsome faces.

At this rate, I'll flunk Witchcraft 101. I want to hunt down the bastards that destroyed my future, but the brothers' past is threatening to steal my soul and tear me apart—literally.

To survive, I must embrace the darkness simmering inside me and unleash the devil within, no matter the consequences...

PICK UP YOUR COPY NOW!
http://bit.ly/buyshadowwalker

www.ingramcontent.com/pod-product-compliance
Lightning Source LLC
Chambersburg PA
CBHW051430170626
46809CB00006B/2399